That evenin sticky. Was there something about the heat that made us all act crazy that night? Was it a full moon? Or, was it the exhilaration of making our exit from high school and starting our journey to the unknown? Whatever the reason, Frankie, Sam, Marcia, and I were destined for a night that would change all four of our lives forever.

The Price of Secrets

by

Jacquie May Miller

The Price of Secrets

Cover Art by *Jennifer Greeff*

The Wild Rose Press, Inc.
PO Box 708
Adams Basin, NY 14410-0708
Visit us at www.thewildrosepress.com

Publishing History
First Edition, 2021
Trade Paperback ISBN 978-1-5092-3548-3
Digital ISBN 978-1-5092-3549-0

Published in the United States of America

Dedication

In memory of my dad, Jack May.
His love of literature and penchant for writing
inspired me to take my thoughts
and turn them into stories.
Love you, Dad.

Chapter One
Coming Home

If I had known I was going to die today, I would have chosen my underwear more carefully. Had my mother been around to help me dress this morning, she would have gladly offered her sage advice, something about looking my best in case I were in an accident. I might end up in a hospital or, God forbid, on the coroner's table, so I should always be prepared. But Mom wasn't here, so instead of the creamy silk camisole that once caressed my younger, smoother skin, I'd pulled my faded jeans and my old Cal Berkeley hooded sweatshirt over my well-worn undergarments and was now about to suffer the consequences of my mother's, apparently correct, advice. Could she have been right about something? I had to give her this one…because I knew in my heart of hearts that this was it. Today was the day I was going to die.

Justin pried my white knuckles from the armrest between us. "It's okay, Mom. Just breathe."

Had I forgotten to breathe? At Justin's insistence, I took in a big gulp of stale, recirculated air and coughed, keeping my words and fears to myself. When he tried to let go of my hand, I twisted my fingers into a tight grip—if he wouldn't let me hold the armrest, I'd be damned if I'd let him remove my only lifeline—I needed to hold onto something. Keeping his hand captive, I leaned into him wondering why I'd let him share this journey. He chose to be by my side on this occasion and now his life was in danger, too. We were both going to die.

Then the announcement came, "This is your captain speaking. No, Jamie, you are *not* going to die, we're just experiencing some minor turbulence." Did he actually say my name? Of course, he didn't. The glass of wine I'd downed just before boarding must have impaired my senses—but, sadly, the alcohol had done little to quell my fear of flying. Still, the message got through—the captain assured me he had this baby under control—I was probably not going to die on this day.

God, I hated flying. Was that why I hadn't been back to Seattle in twenty-five years?

Justin gently pushed my head off his shoulder and freed himself from my surprisingly tight grip. He fanned his fingers, flexing them to get the circulations going again. "The worst is over. We're up in the air now."

"And you think telling me we're up in the air is supposed to make me feel better?" I managed to eke out a ragged laugh. "Anyway, I'm sorry for the physical abuse. Is your hand okay?" I touched his red knuckles wondering how my small fingers could make such a mark. "Thanks for snapping me out of my spiraling thoughts of doom and gloom."

"No problem. Maybe another glass of wine would help."

"Not sure that's a good idea. I might be drunk by the time we reach Seattle."

He shook his head as he laughed, mocking me with

his soft brown eyes. "You're such a lightweight. I gotta say, though, I've never seen you like this."

"Yeah, I'm the kick-ass woman who's always in control." I couldn't believe my reaction myself. It took a lot to rattle me.

"Kick-ass is putting it mildly. I'm glad I've never pissed you off."

I smiled for the first time since takeoff. "I wouldn't go that far."

Justin narrowed his eyes with fake indignation. "Seriously, Mom, I'm surprised you never went back to give your mother a piece of your mind. Was she really that scary?"

"Yeah, yeah. I know you think I'm a tough cookie, but I wasn't so tough at seventeen. And yes, she was that scary." My childhood flashed through my mind. "No one ever won an argument with my mother."

"I don't remember winning too many with you, Mom."

"I think you have a short memory. In my mind, I let you win a few too many." I laughed. "But really, our disagreements were nothing compared to the wrath of Nancy Madison. I couldn't hold a candle to your grandma."

"I guess you weren't so bad." Justin smiled as he dished out the backhanded compliment. "I probably wasn't the easiest kid, and you didn't have any backup for the first couple of years."

"You weren't so bad yourself, kiddo." Those two years had been tough, but in spite of our struggles, or maybe because of them, we forged a special bond. I was one lucky mom.

"Are you sure it's the flight that's getting to you?

Maybe it's what's on the ground at the other end," Justin said.

"Maybe…" I whispered. He knew me so well.

Despite my protest, Justin ordered wine for me and a beer for himself. I laid my head back realizing it surely was the destination rather than the flight that had my ass. I wouldn't have to face my mother, but Dad was another story. After all these years, I still did not understand why he'd severed communication, virtually removing me from his life. Mom was the boss, for sure, but Dad could have found a way to keep in touch—he didn't. In a few days, if I could muster the nerve to face him, I'd ask him why.

It was almost surreal thinking about going home to Seattle, that is, if you could call the place I spent my first seventeen years, home. I leaned over Justin toward the small window to see San Francisco shrink to a barely visible blip under the sporadic, buttermilk clouds. More than half of my life had unfolded in the Bay Area, Berkeley, to be exact. That was truly my home now. Seattle was my old life—my very old life.

But here I was, on my way back after a twenty-five-year absence. I suppose I could have returned anytime by car or bus or train if I was so damned afraid to fly. But Justin was right. Flying was not the issue. I would have loved to use that as an excuse, but the truth was, I had been told—and not so nicely—to get my ass out of Seattle and *never* come back. Never is a long time…and since the woman who arranged my exile was no longer around, I was coming back!

I could have avoided the exile. My mother, Nancy Madison, made it very clear that the choice was simple: I could have an abortion, or I could leave home forever.

I chose the latter, agreeing to keep my mouth shut and never show my face in Seattle again. That woman offered me nothing in return for my silence, but in my teenage naivety, I accepted her proposition and never looked back—until today.

"Are you okay?" Justin waved his hand in front of my face as he reached toward the flight attendant to take the drinks we'd ordered. "You look like you're a million miles away."

"Twenty-five years away really. I was just thinking about my exit from Seattle."

"It must have been hard for you losing your parents so suddenly. And now you've lost your mom forever."

"I'd already lost her. Her death just makes it final. It's so damn unfair she got such an easy exit after the years of misery she created for the rest of us." I thought about the call from my sister, Sarah, almost three months ago telling me Mom had died—a stroke had taken her down as she pulled into the driveway after a trip to the mall. She announced her own death as her head fell forward, causing the horn to stick in a loud, continuous blast. Dad, of course, responded to the summons, wondering what the hell she wanted this time. For once she didn't want anything—she would never want anything again.

"I'm glad I never met her." Justin said the words, but his tone was vague and hesitant. Was he truly glad he hadn't met her? Maybe he would have been the one to turn her cold heart around.

I stared at the wine and the open package of peanuts on my tray table, trying to decide if the aroma of stale peanuts was more enticing than the prospect of numbing my brain with more alcohol. "I seriously thought she'd live forever and, as odd as it sounds, I thought I'd see my mother again. Maybe I should have reached out to her."

"Are you kidding? She was a cold-hearted bitch who threw you out when you were only seventeen. She's the one who should have reached out to you."

Justin had such a strong sense of morality—just the opposite of my mother. He cared about people and right now that was evident in his compassion for me. It was a reciprocal arrangement. We'd seen each other through so many difficult times and today it was his turn to hold me up. He knew I'd do the same for him.

"I can always count on you, Justin. I'm so glad you're here with me. I love you so much—you do know that, don't you?"

"Of course, I do. I love you, too, Mom."

****

Even after all these years, I'd never shared all the details of my departure from Seattle—how could I tell him his grandmother suggested abortion. His limited version of the story ended with my mom's ultimatum to get myself and my swollen belly out of town before anyone was the wiser. He didn't know my one act of defiance against my mother saved his life—and the choice to save his life…saved mine.

"Are you sure you're okay, Mom?"

I inhaled a dose of the stifling airplane air and sucked in a healthy swig of wine. "You know, I think I *am* okay. I'm a little nervous about facing my past but, damn it, I've been through worse."

"So why are you going back?"

Why was I going back? Did I want to face Justin's father? Did I want to see my own father? Yes, and yes—I wanted to make peace with both my dad and Justin's dad. I just wasn't sure how much I wanted to share with my son about his biological father.

"I want to see my old neighborhood and spend some time with my sister. Sarah's been the only link to my old life all these years and now I can actually visit her in Seattle instead of waiting for her to come to us." I'd always cherished the fact that my sister, Sarah, went behind Mom's back and kept in touch with me from the day I left, right up to today. I was looking forward to spending the next two weeks with her.

"That will be nice. I love Aunt Sarah and Uncle David." Justin's eyes bored into mine. "But be honest, Mom. I know this is more than a vacation for you with your big high school reunion. How is that going to feel after all this time?"

"I wasn't sure I'd ever go back, but I'm not going to let my mother keep me away one minute longer." I took another sip of wine hoping to achieve the relaxation the first glass had failed to accomplish. "I know that must seem weird. I haven't seen these people since high school. I'm sure they all think I fell off the face of the earth, but I need to go. I need to let a few people know I had no choice."

"Is my biological father one of those *few people*?" Justin turned his face toward to window. "I mean, you did tell me my father was someone from high school. Did you ever want to tell him about me?"

"I thought about it every day, but I promised my mom I wouldn't tell. If I told your father, it would get back to the neighborhood and all of Mom's friends. She wanted me to fall off the radar and keep our little secret. Mom, Dad, and Sarah were the only people from my old life who knew about you." I touched Justin's chin with its two-day stubble of dark brown whiskers and gently turned his face back in my direction. "I'm sorry, Justin. It wasn't fair to you or to him, but I didn't know what else to do at the time." And after all these years, was it too late to share my son with this man? What would he say when he found out his son had been kept from him for over twenty-four years? "Do you want to meet your dad?"

Justin and I locked our matching brown eyes on one another, and he spoke more sharply than a child should speak to his mother. "I met my dad when I was two years old. When you married Paul and he adopted me, you gave me the best father a kid could ever wish for. As far as I'm concerned, he was, and is, the only guy I'll ever call Dad."

I flinched under the eyes of passengers across the aisle. We'd been speaking quietly, but Justin's love for Paul Crandall increased the intensity of his already deep tone. I lowered my voice. "I can't disagree with that. But maybe it's time for you to meet your biological father."

Justin took my cue and brought his words to a more private decibel. "I don't need to meet the guy who knocked you up. I wonder about him at times, but I'm not sure I want to meet him. If you ran away, he must have been a jerk. Was he?"

"No. I mean, I don't know. It wouldn't have worked out. Between my mom and an immature eighteen-year-old boy, I didn't have much of a future back home." I closed my eyes imagining how things might have looked if I'd stayed home. "I'm glad I took my scholarship to Cal Berkeley and left Seattle behind.

I got a good education, had a beautiful son, and met Paul. I couldn't have asked for more."

"Yes, you could have. You could have asked for more years with Dad." Justin pulled his sunglasses out of his pocket and quickly covered his eyes. His voice cracked. "It's been five years and I still miss him so much. I wish I'd been there when the fire broke out. Maybe I could have saved him."

"There was nothing you could have done." It was my turn to comfort him—so hard since I still felt the ache of Paul's loss every day. I gently removed his sunglasses and touched the tear that mirrored mine. "I'm glad you were away at school. What would I have done if I lost both of you?"

"Oh, Mom, I'm not going anywhere. I may not live with you anymore, but you know I'd do anything for you."

"I know. You're here, aren't you? How did you get out of work?"

"I had some vacation coming and I figured you needed some moral support."

"Thanks, kiddo. You're right, I have no doubt I could have done this alone, but glad you're here."

Leaning back for a moment, I closed my eyes—maybe I could take a short nap—the wine was starting to send a message to my body. Ahhh, I could finally relax.

The respite was short-lived as the plane dropped and jerked, violently, in my opinion. The captain had lied to me—we *were* going to die! I couldn't unfasten my seatbelt fast enough as I jumped up to survey the other passengers who I assumed would be donning their oxygen masks. Thank God the seat next to me was unoccupied, allowing me to lean, somewhat unsteadily, toward the couple across from us. As I peered down the aisle, I noticed that except for one distressed woman with a crying baby, no one was visibly panicked, in fact, most everyone was sitting calmly, watching movies on their phones, reading, or lying back for the nap I coveted. All except Justin who had to grab my wine as I bashed my knee on my tray table.

Between Justin's booming voice and my acrobatics, the couple across the aisle couldn't seem to keep their eyes on their own business. The woman's lips were so tight and her eyes so narrow, I swore I was looking at my dead mother—judging me again. The man, who I assumed was her husband, seemed to be trying to match his wife's disgust, but his hand over his mouth failed to disguise the fact he was laughing. Poor guy reminded me of my dad—he was surely destined for a "talking to" when he got home. Normally, I would have cared what those people thought, but not today. I really didn't give a damn.

What was wrong with me? Whether it was the flight or the resurgence of memories of my husband, Paul, I just couldn't shake the lump in my throat.

I sat back down and turned to Justin, taking the wine and pouring the last gulp down my throat. We talked—a little more quietly this time to avoid the evil-eye across the aisle—sharing a few details of our personal lives. What a lucky mom I was to have a son willing to share both his sorrow and his hope for a better future. Maybe I'd feel that hope again one day. When we ran out of words, I reached over the arm dividing us and pulled him in for a hug. We both needed to hold onto someone right now as we thought of Paul and how our lives had changed in the past five years. Loosening my grip, I finally exhaled. "Love you, kiddo."

Justin nodded, and as he leaned back displaying his distinctive profile, I surveyed the features of my little boy—now not so little and no longer a boy. He looked like me with no hint of his father's features. Every day I looked for a sign of his biological father—the shape of his nose (all mine, unfortunately), the shape and color of his eyes (mine), his dark chestnut-brown mop of hair (mine, again), his smile and giggly laugh (definitely mine)—but there was no trace of his father's heritage. I had hoped it would be clear as the years passed, but the only thing that was clear after twenty-five years was that I did not know who Justin's father was—Frankie or Sam.

Chapter Two
Home at Last

I survived the flight, underwear intact, but wasn't sure I was going to survive the ride in the puny, lime-green Ford Fiesta. Could I have possibly requested this car? I don't think so, but it appeared to be the last available "mid-sized" vehicle in the rental car fleet. It was either this or a giant SUV at twice the price, so we settled on the economy ride. Justin drove the thirty-mile trek from Sea-Tac Airport to Sarah's house, darting between lanes in Seattle's rush hour traffic. Gutsy would be an overstatement of the green machine's performance, but it had more pizzazz than I expected and got us to my sister Sarah's front door in one piece. The coroner and the paramedics were denied a peek at my pathetic underwear—all my worry about dying today had been for naught.

Seeing Sarah in the doorway in her yellow, cotton sundress reminded me the trip was worth every turbulent air pocket I'd endured. My sister had been my only link to family for almost twenty-five years and I was finally able to see her on her turf—my old turf. Only five miles north of our childhood home, Sarah's house, a cute, yellow rambler with flowerpots full of geraniums built into the windowsill, reflected her personality. I felt a sense of peace the moment I stepped out of the car, not just because the ride was over, but because I was in the calm presence of my older, wiser sister. What a change from our younger days.

"Hey, Jamie!" Sarah ran out to the car as I ran toward her and we hugged for what seemed like a full minute. Justin stood beside us impatiently.

"Sarah, it's so good to see you. I can't believe I'm really here."

"I can't either," Justin cut in, reminding us he was here, too. "Aunt Sarah, it's great to see you, but I think I should leave you two alone to talk. Okay if I take the car, Mom?"

"Okay, kiddo. But first, you can help me take our bags in."

Sarah guided us to our rooms—the frilly guest room was mine. Justin would spend the next two weeks in his cousin Mark's slightly less appealing room papered with video game posters and laden with sports trophies from kindergarten T-ball to college baseball. After delivering the bags to our quarters, Justin ran out to the living room to give his aunt a quick hug before running out the door. I heard his text tone as he was leaving.

Sarah's mouth was wide open as she watched him escape. "What was that all about?"

"He's got a new girlfriend." I couldn't help giggling as I watched him trip over the welcome mat— catching himself and leaping off the porch. "She's from Seattle, but she's been hired by his company and will be moving to San Francisco in a couple of weeks. He seems pretty smitten with her. She's a techno-geek like him."

"Wow, I don't remember him ever being so enthusiastic, at least not recently." Sarah smiled and raised an eyebrow. "I hope he has a good time."

"Not too good, I hope. I don't want him to do what I did. I'm much too young to be a grandma."

"You can't stop them, Jamie. He's twenty-four for God's sake. Let them have some fun."

"I think he would, but it sounds like she has a stronger moral compass than my boy and is keeping him at arm's length." I laughed. "I like her already."

"I know you're the careful one—except for that one night—but let your son find some joy. He isn't stupid. I assume he knows about condoms."

"So he says. I guess I'm just overprotective. The last few years have been tough." I looked away.

"I'm sorry, Jamie." She grabbed my hand and led me to the kitchen where she poured us both a glass of wine. "I wasn't thinking. Of course, it's been hard for both of you losing Paul."

"I know I should move on—and Justin, too—but it's not that easy." I took a gulp of the wine as I plopped my tired body on the barstool and leaned on the counter. "I'm getting there, though. I know life goes on."

"Is that why you decided to come back to Seattle? I mean, why now? Why is this the right time to confront Frankie and Sam?" She sat across from me on a kitchen stool.

"Besides the obvious?" My eyes were wide with disbelief as I stared at Sarah. "You do remember Mom just died, right? I may be forty-two years old, but she still scared the shit out of me. I never would have come back if she were still alive."

"Really, Jamie?" Sarah's voice had an accusatory tone—but, maybe that was just my thin skin.

"You knew Mom better than anyone, Sarah. What would she have done if all her friends and relatives found out about Justin—my 'illegitimate' son? I didn't have the nerve to defy her, even after all these years."

Sarah smiled a knowing smile. "You're probably right, Sis. She wouldn't want her daughter's dirty little secret smearing her in the eyes of her friends." Sarah knew exactly what I was talking about. "But back to the original question: How are you going to tell Frankie and Sam?"

"I'm not sure I'll tell them right away. I just want to know—I mean—in case Justin ever wants to trace his roots." I wasn't sure myself why I so desperately wanted to determine the identity of Justin's biological father. No one needed a kidney or anything.

"You always told me you didn't want or need to know. What changed your mind?"

"It's time. Justin deserves the truth. Besides, I'm tired of hiding."

"Are you sure you want to do this?"

"Sarah, I just want a normal life again. The last few years without Paul have been tough, and I've spent a lot of lonely nights glued to the internet looking up old friends. After twenty-five years, I can't just send someone a friend request on Facebook—not after leaving without a word to anyone. But I'd really like to see some of those people, and when I saw on the classmates' site that we were having a high school reunion, I thought this might be my chance."

"It's not going to be easy after all this time, Jamie."

"I know. I already got a strange message from the reunion committee when I signed up." I smiled thinking of the note even though it truly wasn't that funny.

"They thought I'd passed away and wanted to know if they should remove my name from the list of deceased schoolmates."

Sarah laughed. We both had a pretty sick sense of humor and when she launched her infectious cackle, complete with snorting, it got me going, too. It felt good to giggle with my sister again—it seemed as if no time had passed. For the first time in five years, the tears rolling down my cheeks were born of laughter rather than sorrow. So good to be home.

Sarah went to the sink, pulled off a couple of paper towels, and handed me one to wipe the tears clinging to my cheeks. The rough material felt like sandpaper on my sensitive skin, but it did the job—or did it?

"You look like a raccoon." Sarah snorted again.

We both took a deep breath and a swig of our wine. In a few minutes, we were finally able to talk again.

"Sarah, do you think it's too late. Will Sam and Frankie hate me when they find out I've kept this from them?"

"That's a chance you'll have to take. I know you, Jamie, and you'll always feel guilty if you don't tell them. If you wait any longer, it will only feel worse. Just get it over with—pull the Band-Aid off that old wound and let it start healing."

"Yeah, I know I'll feel better, no matter what the outcome. They're probably pissed at me already for deserting them. What's one more little surprise? How much madder could they get?"

Sarah's gaze was steady. "You are kidding, right? I think you're going to have some angry boys on your hands, but you've got to do it. They deserve to know."

My head was starting to ache as I sat the wine on

the counter. "Hey, let's not talk about this anymore." I rubbed my raccoon eyes and leaned back. "Tell me what's going on with you. I know Mark moved out last year, but where's Eric? Doesn't he come home for summer break?"

"He had to lease his apartment in Pullman for a full year, so he decided to take some classes summer semester. I think he likes being three hundred miles away from us."

"So, you're an empty nester like me now. How does that feel?" Her head bowed as her eyes closed. Had I struck a nerve—was she about to cry? Then she looked up, her hazel eyes sparkling; her lips curled in a wicked grin.

"It feels wonderful! I love my boys but having the run of the house with my sexy husband is the best. Besides, the boys are ready to cut the cord."

"How nice for you and David. I loved my empty nest, too…until Paul died." When Justin packed his bags for Stanford, I cried my heart out, but Paul and I adjusted quite nicely after a few months. Now my nest was totally empty, and I was crying again. "I can't seem to control my tears today."

"It's okay, Jamie. Should I refill your wine glass?"

I pushed the glass in her direction. "No, please take what's left away. The wine is just making me sleepy and weepy. I hope you don't mind if just make myself a sandwich and go to bed."

"No problem, Sis. I'll save the chicken for tomorrow." She hugged me as I walked around the counter into the kitchen. Then she reached into the cupboard and handed me my drug of choice—peanut butter—she remembered my childhood favorite.

We talked a little more as I made my peanut butter and jelly sandwich and poured myself a glass of milk—that's what I needed. The aroma of peanut butter transported me to Mom's kitchen and reminded me I once felt loved and nurtured by the woman who threw me out. Hard to believe that woman could still pull at my heartstrings even from the grave. I sighed after the last bite and turned toward the guest room.

"See you in the morning, Sarah. Love you." I squeezed her hand across the counter.

"If you want to get up at the crack of dawn, I'll see you. If not, I'll see you after your little pre-reunion cocktail party tomorrow night. Love you, too, little sis."

As tired as I was, the sleep I craved was delayed by premonitions of the days ahead. Would Frankie or Sam be at the cocktail party tomorrow? If so, what would I say to them? After all these years, what could I say? I rehearsed all the possible opening lines: *Hi, boys, are either of you looking to add a twenty-four-year-old son to your family?* Or maybe, *remember when I ran away twenty-five years ago—well I forgot to tell you something.* Maybe I would just say hello and leave the rest of the details for later.

My heart was beating faster as I thought of my personal reunion with these guys, but I knew I wouldn't run away this time. I was ready to face the music even if I encountered a few sour notes. Carry on, I thought, and immediately the words to that song implanted themselves in my mind. *If you're lost and alone and sinking like a stone, carry on. Carry on, carry on.* And for the next two hours as I tried to sleep, the words haunted me until I finally sank like a stone into a restless sleep.

Chapter Three
Cheers

They didn't see me in the corner. I'd chosen a spot that kept my image in profile—an image certain to keep me from easy recognition. Was it too late to escape? Should I have slipped out before they noticed me? No. Even though I feared reuniting with old friends, I knew I had to do this.

I'd arrived early, securing my place by the bay window, and for the last hour, as I watched the sun sift through the clouds, painting streaks of orange and gold across the summer sky, I willed myself to calm down. As the sun dropped into Puget Sound and the bright hues faded to shades of gray, my perch by the window left me in darker shadows, granting my wish for anonymity.

No bright lights or name tags tonight—the official reunion Saturday night promised all the glitz, complete with music, dancing, and our best party dresses. Tonight, at this waterfront bar overlooking Puget Sound, the entertainment was limited to a big screen TV showing the Seattle Mariners baseball game and a dartboard in the corner. But that's not why we were here. This Thursday night pre-function offered an opportunity for a more casual chat with old friends and a chance for connection with those who couldn't afford the ridiculous cost of the reunion dinner/dance.

As classmates started filing into the small bar, I realized I only recognized a few. Balding guys with beer guts and women wearing too much makeup to hide wrinkles earned over the past twenty-five years moved into the room with wide eyes and tentative steps. Others who seemed to have survived the years with minimal damage, marched in with more jaunty strides and faces glowing with confidence. Being one of the younger classmates at age forty-two, I'd had less time to age and I'd say I fell into the category of the well-preserved, although I was not as self-assured as some of my classmates seemed to be. Even with a little help from the surgeon's knife after the fire, I still lacked total faith in my appearance. But…I was here. Five years ago, I wouldn't have shown my scarred left cheek and ear to anyone, but today my face looked better than it did in high school. Maybe it was cheating, but as long as I was under anesthesia, I opted for a little sculpting on my oversized nose—something I'd always wanted to do but definitely wouldn't have made a special trip for the procedure. Was it enough of a change to keep from being recognized? Probably not, but enough to make me wonder why I'd felt the need. My good genes had done most of the work, keeping the gray from my dark, chestnut brown hair and my petite frame slim, although the weight management was partly due to the stress of the past five years. They say the eyes are the windows to one's soul, and I had to say, my dark brown eyes were the windows to the Jamie Madison of high school. My sunglasses were covering them, but now that it was dark, the shades would have to go.

As the crowd swelled, the two boys who had once meant so much to me drifted closer to my table. When they glanced my way, I turned toward the window avoiding eye contact—I wasn't ready to talk. With no hint of recognition, I felt safe with a half-turn to observe the men I'd thought about so often over the years. Frankie had changed the least, still the swarthy, dark Italian with a look I could never resist. But Sam was nearly unrecognizable—in a very good way—his once short, nondescript brown hair now a thick mass of longer silver-streaked locks. Neither Frankie nor Sam had ever been considered quiet, so I heard every word of their conversation.

"What the hell are you doing here, Sam? Haven't seen you since the ten-year reunion." Frankie took a hefty swig of what looked like coke, but from my memory of Frankie, I assumed there was a double shot of whiskey in the mix. He waited for a response from his old friend—or were they still friends after that night so long ago?

"I travel a lot, but my business schedule brought me back to Seattle this week, so I thought I'd check it out." Sam was taking it slower with his beer, just like the old days, a careful approach to everything. "Do you and Marcia always come to these things?"

"Well, Marcia and I are getting a divorce, but yeah, we always came to the reunions—Ten, Fifteen, Twenty, and now Twenty-five. I think Marcia liked to relive her glory days when she was the most popular girl in school."

"Sorry, man, I didn't know you two were splitting up."

"Don't be sorry. She's been a pain in the ass from day one. I'm here to celebrate." Frankie raised his glass and Sam met him halfway to toast the demise of the marriage.

I could have told Frankie that Marcia was a pain in the ass. Oh, yeah, I did tell him about a thousand times from middle school through high school. Frankie and I had been friends since the day he moved into the neighborhood at age twelve. I had a crush on that bad boy the minute he stepped out of the moving truck with his Aunt Betty. Black leather and long hair created an image we hadn't seen in our cozy little neighborhood, but it was a look that got my attention. And through the years of our friendship and eventually much more, my warnings of Marcia Jensen's shallow, selfish ways landed on deaf ears. Her pouty lips, cornflower blue eyes, and long, blonde hair trumped any shortcomings in her personality. Or was it her perfectly formed "D" cup breasts—they likely didn't hurt her cause.

Sam put a hand on Frankie's shoulder. "So, if Marcia didn't drag you to the reunion this year, why are you here?"

Frankie pulled away from Sam. "I'm single now. Maybe it's time for me to relive my glory days. There were a few girls who would have looked my way if I hadn't been taken."

I wondered if he was sorry he'd been "taken." I was the one who'd done the taking back then, but he was the one who convinced me we were a good match. There were always girls hitting on him, not just Marcia. No one could believe he'd want to spend his time with a bookish, nerdy girl like me. I was cute, but Marcia was beautiful. Frankie could have had "beautiful," but he chose someone with a little more heart and soul—he chose me. Was it because I knew where he came from? The sadness I still saw behind his sexy, dark eyes reminded me of his heart-wrenching story. From age twelve to the day I left, he had trusted me, and only me, with the whole story of his tortured childhood, and I couldn't help wondering if he'd shared it with anyone else once I left? Even after all the shit that happened between us later, I hoped he'd found peace with his past.

Sam laughed—a little too loud—reminding me more of the old high school kid than this new, improved version of Sam I looked at now. "I don't have to worry about that. I doubt if there are even ten girls who would remember me and that's only if the Science Club shows up."

Frankie nodded, obviously remembering Sam's awkward ways. "But somehow you got the attention of my girlfriend. I never could figure out what Jamie saw in you."

"Ouch. Still the same tactful guy." Sam looked Frankie straight in the eye. "Apparently, *your* girlfriend found my brain attractive. But it doesn't matter at this point. She hasn't talked to me in twenty-five years. Do you ever hear from her?"

"Never. She went off to Berkeley and never looked back."

Frankie was wrong, I had looked back. I called Sarah every week to find out what those boys were up to. I missed them both—my dear friend and study buddy, Sam Bradley, and the boy I had loved so long, Frankie Angelo. Neither one deserved to be an instant father, but even if one of them would have been a perfect partner and Dad, I had promised my mother to keep this secret. True to my moral upbringing, I always kept my promises. Looking at these two great guys now, I wondered if I'd made a mistake. How self-sacrificing I had been to save them from the burden of fatherhood, and how cruel and self-serving to deprive them of the joy of knowing Justin. All these years I passed the blame to my Mom—after all, she set the rules—I was merely following them. No more! Now it was time to break the rules and end my long silence. It was time to find out which one of these men was Justin's father...

Marcia was across the room, eyeing Frankie—or was she looking at Sam? As she headed our direction, strutting her slightly rounder ass proudly across the room, I knew it was time for me to make my move. For once I would beat Marcia to her target. It took me twenty-five years, but tonight I would steal her thunder—I would be the star. Hard to believe I still felt the pain of her rejection so many years ago and harder to believe that I wanted to prove, even twenty-five years later, that I was just as good as Marcia Jensen.

Sliding off my stool, I replaced my sunglasses with the glasses I still needed to see beyond my nose. At least now it was fashionable to wear glasses, so my popularity would not be in jeopardy as it had been in high school. Moving my smaller, cuter ass quickly toward the boys, I cut Marcia off seconds before she had a chance to open her pouty mouth. I looked at Frankie first. God, he was handsome—those dark, Italian eyes with the thick, black lashes still had the power to melt me. The deep wrinkles around those eyes revealed the strain of his years with Marcia, but in a way, they added to his appeal. He looked a little rough and worn, but he was all man and I remembered why I'd fallen so hard way back when.

Then, I looked at Sam. Wow, what happened to him? He was so tall and built like a Greek god. The definition of his pecs under his polo shirt did not resemble anything I'd seen on the puny kid I'd known in high school. Little Sammy Bradley had grown up and even if he was still a science geek, on the surface he was quite a hottie. Now I knew why Marcia was on her way over. She was done with Frankie, so why not take a crack at my other male interest, Sam, the same Sam she laughed at in high school. I could only hope he would laugh at her this time. But it was my turn to face these boys first.

As I entered their space, I kept my head down and my voice low. I may have altered my tone a bit. "Hi, boys."

"Do we know you?" Frankie asked.

I looked up and straight into his eyes as my voice returned to its normal timber. "You know me all right. I think I was your first friend in the neighborhood, Frankie Angelo."

"Oh my God, Jamie, is that really you? You look different, but I'd recognize your voice anywhere."

"And those eyes..." Sam chimed in. "You can change your face, but you can't change those big, brown eyes. But why did you change your face, Jamie?"

"I didn't have a lot of choice in the matter—except for the nose—I figured if they were in there fixing my scars, they could make me a better nose."

Sam looked closely. "It's cute, but I liked your old nose." He looked at me with a furrowed brow. "Scars? What..." He obviously wanted to ask me what happened, but Frankie cut in.

"Well, I like it. I think you look great, Jamie." Frankie was always full of compliments. Did he mean it this time? And did he even wonder why I had the surgery? Did he care?

"Thanks, guys. It's really good to see you two." And it was.

"But I'm not letting you off the hook that easy," Frankie said, "Where the hell have you been these past twenty-five years? I tried to get it out of your sister, Sarah, and she just said she was sworn to secrecy. What was that all about?"

"I knew I could count on Sarah. It's a long story, guys, but let's just say my sister was there when I needed her."

Sam reached for my hand and I willingly allowed him to wrap my fingers in his warm grip. "I'm sorry if I let you down, Jamie. Could we have helped you?"

"Yes, Jamie," Marcia added as she wormed her way into the inner circle, "What could we have done?"

"You, Marcia, have done enough to last a lifetime. You're probably the biggest reason I stayed in California for twenty-five years."

Frankie stepped between me and Marcia, trying to avert the catfight he saw coming. It was tempting—I wanted to shake that woman and make her pay for all the pain she'd inflicted on everyone in her path. But the truth was, I owed her a debt of gratitude for orchestrating the incident that finally pushed me away. Life hadn't been so bad in Berkeley, in fact, if I'd stayed in Seattle, I might never have met my husband, Paul Crandall. The seventeen years we had together were the best years of my life, so despite the heat rising inside me at the mere sight of Marcia Jensen, I wanted to thank her for opening that door.

That was the magnanimous, good-hearted Jamie speaking inside my head. My evil twin wanted nothing more than to see Marcia suffer. After the way she treated me in high school, she deserved some retribution. My life may have worked out the way it should have, but I'd be damned if I would give her the satisfaction of knowing she manipulated me right into a better life.

Marcia obviously didn't take offense at my remark, or maybe she just wanted the last word. "You certainly could have come back anytime, Jamie. We're all your friends. I don't know why you ever thought I didn't like you. My God, we've been friends since grade school."

"Really, Marcia? Did you forget the fact that you quit speaking to a person of my lowly status from seventh grade on? Funny how we forget these little things after twenty-five years." Maybe I had the last word after all.

"I didn't forget, but I didn't forget all the good years we had. I am so ashamed I let those bitchy girls in high school convince me we were better than you."

"You mean those girls across the room that you were just talking to? Are they all coming over to make a tearful apology, too?"

"Oh, Jamie, let's just let the past go. We all grow up eventually. It just takes some of us longer than others." She looked at Frankie as she said those words. "I'm *really* sorry, Jamie."

Was she for real? I wasn't sure, but I had to know if she still had a hold on Frankie. I looked from Marcia to Frankie, then back to Marcia. "So, I heard you two are splitting up. Any truth to that rumor?"

"It's all true. You came back just in time—he's all yours! I don't know why we were ever in competition for this guy. He didn't turn out to be as cool as his black leather jacket made him look."

"What she's trying to say," Frankie interjected looking directly at Marcia, "is that looks aren't everything. I totally agree, Marcia. A beautiful face doesn't guarantee a kind heart or a functioning brain."

"Don't put words in my mouth. I know you have a brain. Too bad that brain can't find a way to make more money," Marcia chided.

"A teacher's salary isn't that bad. I don't see you adding anything much with your homemade greeting card business, if you can call it a business," Frankie said.

"Hey, I didn't come here to listen to you two go at it," I said as I looked at Frankie. "I must admit, though, I never expected you to become a teacher."

"I think I've changed in a lot of ways you never expected. I don't think you expected much from me."

"That's not true. I expected great things from you—I just wasn't sure you expected much from yourself." His hand brushed against my arm and I felt a rush of heat ascend my spine. Would that feeling ever go away? "I'm glad to see you found a way to go to college."

Sam was about to drift away from our little group. I wasn't ready to let him go, so I grabbed the plate of appetizers from my table behind us. "Hey, guys, help me eat these bacon-wrapped meatballs."

Frankie grabbed one immediately, followed by Marcia, who really didn't need one and wasn't one of the "guys" included in the offer. Sam declined, stating that the fat content was too high, and they were not a healthy choice. Despite my efforts to convince him to enjoy a decadent snack once in a while, he continued to refuse. The rest of us ignored our middle-aged bodies and finished off the unhealthy morsels. I returned the dish to the table and offered to dispose of Frankie's used toothpick. An excuse to touch his hand again.

The touch got his attention—he grabbed my hand. "Hey, Jamie, if you have some time tomorrow, I'd like to come by. I'll take you for a ride to the old neighborhood."

"That would be nice." I guess there was no sense in staying mad at the guy after all these years. "I'll give you Sarah's address."

"Oh, I know where she lives. I've been bugging her for years to tell me where you went."

I didn't know how to react to that. I just needed to get out of there before my heart overtook my good sense. "Well, boys—and Marcia—I need to get going. See you all at the reunion Saturday."

Frankie put his arm around my shoulder and pulled me in. I reached up and completed the hug. It was brief but satisfying.

Sam followed his lead, but his embrace was firmer, warmer, and longer. "God, Jamie, it's good to see you." Our eyes locked, and I couldn't turn away. Had his eyes always been so blue? What happened to that skinny kid with the horn-rimmed glasses I said goodbye to in the summer of 1990?

"You, too, Sam." I turned away from him and walked toward the door. I looked back once to see all three of them still looking at me. I waved and walked out.

Chapter Four
My Best Friend

After too many hours in that air-conditioned bar, the night air felt like a warm blanket. As I reached my rental car, I hesitated, then just kept walking toward the beach, pulling my shoes off as soon as I hit the sand. It was still warm from the uncharacteristically hot Seattle day and as I parked myself on an old piece of driftwood, I dug my toes into the soft, brown grains.

I had a lot to think about. Should I go through with my plan? I wanted to find Justin's father for him, but it was so complicated. What would Justin think of me if he knew I had slept with two men at the age of seventeen? I had never been able to share all the details of his conception. He knew the basics—I'd spent my high school years holding onto my virginity, and once I finally lost it, Justin found his way into my womb. He was right—losing my virginity had a lot to do with his arrival, but he didn't know I had followed the night of my deflowering with an act of retaliation the very next night. I hoped I would never have to tell Justin there were two men, but even worse, how would I ever tell Frankie or Sam that I didn't know which one of them was Justin's father?

"Nice night." I jumped when I heard Sam's voice behind me. I was so engrossed in my thoughts I hadn't heard him walking through the sand.

"God, you scared me, Sam! What are you doing here? Is the party over already?"

"I'm done with the party. I've been hoping to see you for twenty-five years. I'm not going to let you leave again without talking about what happened." He sat next to me on our driftwood bench as we watched the ferry float across the still water.

It was too soon to tell him anything—I would know soon enough and could tell him the definitive truth. Why tell him he "might" be the father of my son. So, I kept to small talk. "You knew I had a scholarship to the University of California at Berkeley. I went off to college, got my degree, and decided to stay down there."

"Without a word to me? I thought we were a couple, but I guess I should have realized I was just a rebound from Frankie. Did you ever care for me, Jamie?"

"You know I did. You were my best friend all through high school. I just never saw us as anything more than friends. I never should have slept with you."

"Was I that bad? You were my first and it was unexpected, but I would have liked a second chance."

I couldn't look him in the eye and kept my gaze on the grains of sand between my toes. "I wouldn't have known good from bad that night. I just needed someone to lean on and you were there. You were always there for me, Sam. I'm sorry I couldn't give you more."

"It's okay. No harm done. We both obviously survived the encounter in the back of my dad's Camaro."

Did he really think there was no harm done? Our lives were irrevocably changed by my decision to sleep

31

with two guys in two days. If I had known who fathered Justin, would it have changed my plans? "I guess we survived, but I wouldn't say we got away unscathed."

"What do you mean by that?"

"Oh, I don't know. I just wish things had been different. I wish I'd have been able to keep in touch with you and everyone else for that matter."

"Been able to? They had phones back then and now we have this thing called the internet. We use it to contact old friends." I finally looked up. I expected to see an angry face, but instead, he was smiling.

"What's so funny?"

"I've spent my entire adult life in the field of information technology and there isn't a person, place, or thing I can't find on my computer...except you. I could never find you, Jamie. You just dropped off the face of the earth."

"That was the plan. And once I got married, it was easy to stay off the radar. Who would be looking for Jamie Crandall?"

"Still married?" I think he was hoping I was divorced like at least half of our classmates. This generation wasn't much for commitment it seemed.

"Widowed." I said it so softly I barely heard it myself. After all this time, I still had a hard time with that word. The word that reminded me that Paul would never kiss me goodnight again. I sometimes wondered how I made it through each day.

"I'm so sorry, Jamie." Sam took my hand for the second time that evening. We sat in silence for what seemed like an hour, but was likely no more than five minutes, my hand feeling warm and protected in his firm yet tender grip. For those few moments, I felt safe and secure. Sam was still my security blanket after all these years…

When he let go of my hand, I prepared myself for the evening's end. But his hand had found a new resting place on my cheek as he took my face in his grasp and leaned down to kiss me—a soft, sensual kiss I would never have expected. Was this my Sam? I couldn't stop myself from responding as I wrapped my arms around him and returned his kiss.

My heart was racing, my head was spinning, my…my…oh, my! What was happening? I found room on his lap, wrapping my legs around his strong loins. He pulled me close, and I felt the man—not the boy—I left so many years ago. My sweet Sam wanted me. I could feel every inch of his manhood pressing against me. How could this be happening? I hadn't had, or even wanted a lover since Paul died, but five years was long enough. For once, my conscience was not my guide and I gave in to the glorious feelings of the moment. Our piece of driftwood was slightly out of sight of the bar crowd and the sun had long since set, so the darkness was our shield. There didn't seem to be any stragglers on the beach, but I looked around to be sure, then reached down to feel the rock-hard desire in him—and I knew I had to have him. My white lace panties were the only obstacle between pleasure and frustration—I removed the lacey encumbrance, released him from his khaki prison, and positioned myself on top of him. We were two lovers embracing on the beach to any stray eye chancing by, my long red skirt hiding the skin-to-skin connection. But when I slipped myself onto the part of his anatomy that made him oh, so deliciously different from me, I couldn't help moaning—it was so much for me to handle, yet it filled the space perfectly. Rocking and swaying, we were soon rolling in the damp sand with seaweed in our hair and sand invading our every orifice as we kept time with the rhythmic sound of the waves bringing the tide closer. We fit. We were in sync with one another, with the night. Little Sammy was all grown up and he brought me more pleasure than I could have imagined. I felt alive again, and as we reached our final climax, my breath escaped audibly—very audibly—if anyone was passing by, we were busted. I laughed. I laughed so hard that Sam was compelled to join me with his loud, geeky laugh. I laughed even harder. What a rush! The sea smelled so sweet, the sand felt warm beneath us and I felt a strong desire to start singing "Come Together." What the hell had just happened?

"Oh my God!" I gasped, "Oh—my—God!" I laid my head on his chest. The feeling of euphoria flowed through my body from my spinning head to my sandy toes. What had I just done? I wasn't planning to sleep with Sam, or anyone, for that matter. It was surprising how natural it felt and how responsive my body had been. It couldn't happen again, though—I wasn't ready to let anyone into my life again. But for now, I would enjoy the afterglow and feel the joy of our union. He wrapped his arms around me, and I felt him shiver.

"I've missed you, Jamie. You were always the girl for me." He touched my face so gently. "Let's go back to my hotel."

"Your hotel? You don't live in Seattle?"

"I just transferred to the San Francisco area a few months ago. I never would have left when I was married, but there's nothing for me here anymore."

"No kids?" I asked.

"Long story, but suffice it to say, 'no kids' is the reason we got divorced. I wanted kids and we tried and tried and tried. Imagine my surprise when I found out she'd been on the pill until the day she had her hysterectomy three years ago." He tensed noticeably. "That was it for me. Secrets and lies have no place in a marriage. Dishonesty is the one thing I cannot tolerate under any circumstance."

"Well, at least you're out of that now." He had left a liar, and now he was here with me, someone who had kept a secret from him for twenty-five years. What would he do when he found out I had kept my son's paternity from him? What if he was Justin's father? Would he ever forgive me? I'd think about that tomorrow—or whenever the results were in. I sat up and leaned on my hands. "About your hotel, I think I better pass. I told Sarah I'd be home early tonight, so we could catch up. I think I already missed early by a few hours."

Sam lived in San Francisco. Damn, that was a little too close for comfort. How could I have a brief encounter with an old friend if he was going to follow me back to my neighborhood? I had expected to spend a week in Seattle and then go back to Berkeley and leave the past behind. That would not be so easy now. I had literally screwed things up with this encounter. But God, it felt so good. I didn't want to hurt Sam again, and I certainly didn't want to feel any more pain when it came to love, so I would have to find a way to tell him that this was a mistake. It was a mistake, wasn't it? In this moment, it seemed right, but I knew in the light of day, I could never continue this love affair. I would not tell him tonight, though. Tonight, I would just feel the joy.

"You are not living up to your 'Little' Sammy Wonder title. You knew that's what my dad used to call you, didn't you?" I laid my hand on his ample package—little definitely didn't describe this man.

"I knew. I always liked your dad, but I could never understand that tag. Is your dad still as goofy as he was back then?"

"I don't know." I closed my eyes and shook my head. "I haven't seen him in twenty-five years."

"What?" He sat up and put his hands on my shoulders. "I thought you were just avoiding me and Frankie. What happened with your dad?"

"It was my mom, actually. Dad was just a casualty of her vicious agenda. I never would have come back if she hadn't died."

"Wow. What did you do that was so horrible? I thought you were the good kid in the family."

"All I can say is my mom and I got into a big fight and she wouldn't back down. She bought my plane ticket to Berkeley and told me if I ever showed my face to her or any of our friends or relatives it would be over her dead body." She called that one. "She died on Mother's Day so here I am. One of these days I'll give you all the gory details, but right now I really don't want to talk about it."

"Sorry to hear that. She was always nice to me. I didn't realize you two had any issues. Are you okay, Jamie?"

"More than okay. I can finally come back and visit my old life. It's strange to think I'll never see her or talk to her, but really, 'good riddance'." I laughed, partly because I wanted to believe it was really that simple, that I no longer cared, and partly to expel the tension I felt when I spoke of her. Making light of it and continuing to close off my feelings was how I made it through each day. Her death offered me a chance to reconnect with my old life, and I couldn't say I was sorry for that opportunity. But was I sorry that she was gone? It was an odd feeling to know I would never have a chance to talk to her again but, honestly, what would I say to the woman who took a big piece of my life from me? Good riddance summed it up. I didn't need that shit in my life.

Sam looked at me a little differently after that comment—no longer the adoring look, but a look of "who the hell is this woman?" He'd never seen this side of me. "That must have been some argument. Are you really glad she's gone?"

"I am," I said more softly than my previous declaration. "I believe I really am."

"Jamie, nothing could be that bad."

"Sam, I would not be talking to you now if she were still here." I touched his cheek. "I'm glad she's gone." I kissed him softly and let him hold me for one more moment. I needed his strong arms around me right now.

The pressure of his embrace was perfect—tight enough for me to feel safe and secure, yet loose enough to give me freedom to relax and just breathe. I thought back to that night in high school in the back of his dad's Chevy, his inexperienced hands exploring unmapped territory and holding on so tight my breath could barely escape. Despite my fears of having the life squeezed out of me like a used-up tube of toothpaste, we made it through that night. Offering Sam a second chance was never in my plan—never. Again, my thoughts went back to childhood and the advice my mother always spouted, that is when she wasn't telling me to wear my best underwear—"Never say never, Jamie. You never know…"

Sam rubbed my arms as the night air started to cool. "I don't care why you're here, Jamie. I'm just glad you're back in my life."

At least an hour had passed, and while I enjoyed the gentle murmur of waves, the sound seemed to be getting louder…and closer. Yes, the water was almost to my sand-covered lace panties. I retrieved them quickly and pulled them over my satisfied crotch. Sam reached for his boxers and khakis, wrinkled and damp with the salty sea air, and I watched with sadness as he confined his magnificent body in the clothes.

"We better get going, Sam."

"I don't want to leave. Will you regret this tomorrow? I can't read you, Jamie."

"I'm not easy to read." How could he read me when I couldn't read myself? I picked up my shoes and purse and started walking.

Sam and I walked to the parking lot arm in arm, smoothing our wrinkled garments as we tried to sneak to our cars without detection from any of our old high school classmates. It didn't work. The minute we climbed up from the beach, we were on display under the lamp post, and not twenty feet away, Frankie and Marcia were deep in conversation. For a divorcing couple, they seemed to be joined at the hip.

"Why are you going over to see Jamie tomorrow? Why aren't we all getting together?" Marcia yelled.

"Marcia, you know you and Jamie haven't been friends since middle school. Besides, *I* want to see Jamie. Did you forget you left me? Why do you give a damn what I do? Do you want me back now that Jamie's here to give you a little competition?"

"Of course not. We've been fighting for twenty-four years. Why would I want you back?"

Frankie took her hand. "Maybe because you love me. And you didn't have to fight with me every goddamn day. Why are you so unhappy, Marcia? You've gotten everything you wanted your entire life and you're never satisfied. What the hell do you want?"

Marcia—tough as nails, Marcia—started to cry. "I don't know, Frankie. I don't know. I better get out of here before I do something stupid." She pulled her hand free, turned, and walked to her car.

Frankie stood there watching her as we tried to stay out of his view and sneak to our respective cars. No such luck.

"Hey, Jamie. Hey, Sam. I thought you two had gone home. What have you been doing all this time?" He looked at us from head to toe. Were my shoes on the right feet? Was my hair okay? I looked over and noticed Sam's fly was unzipped. We were busted.

We spoke at the same time. I said, "Just talking."

Sam proclaimed in a louder than necessary voice, "Nothing!"

"Really?" Frankie looked at Sam. "So, you're stealing my girl again, huh?"

"Like I told you earlier, Frankie, I don't think she wants either of us." Sam may have been fishing, but I didn't dare say anything.

Laughing seemed like the right response. "Yeah,

Frankie, I had my fill of you two in high school. Why would I subject myself to that again?" I ran my fingers through my hair and straightened my skirt and then ran over to Frankie and gave him a quick hug. "See you tomorrow at one." I started to walk away.

He pulled me closer and kissed my cheek. "I can't wait to talk to you alone. Goodnight, kiddo."

Why did he have to use that word? He had called me kiddo since we were twelve years old, and as we grew older, I always thought that was his way of telling me he loved me. He wasn't good at saying the words, but when he called me "kiddo," I knew I was his girl. This was going to be a tough weekend. So many memories of that summer long ago and so much I needed to confess about the gift I received nine months later. What would these boys—now men—think when they found out what I had kept from them for twenty-five years?

"Goodnight, Frankie." I waved as he got into his car and drove off.

"Now it's my turn." Sam didn't stop at my cheek but kissed me full on—another sensual arousing kiss. "I hope I won't be second fiddle to Frankie again. It looks like he still has a thing for you, Jamie. Or, should I call you 'kiddo'?"

Looking up into his bluest of blue eyes, I felt like I was seeing him for the first time. "Jamie will do." I reached down and zipped his fly, feeling the growing organ as I gave it one last squeeze. Did I want to let him go? I would be thinking of him all night; that much I knew for sure. I couldn't resist one more kiss. Standing on tiptoes, I pulled him close and kissed him as though it was our last, lingering on his sweet lips long enough

to know this was something special. "Goodnight, Sam."
I touched his cheek as I slipped into the driver's seat of
my car.

Chapter Five
Remembering the Past

As I drove away from the new Sam, I turned the radio on to keep my mind from dwelling on the events of the night. They were playing an old Beatles song "I Should Have Known Better." I felt the warm, damp remnants of our lovemaking in my lace panties and wondered if *I* should have known better. So much for music soothing my soul and keeping my mind quiet. What was I thinking when I turned his kiss into a sexual encounter—a mind-blowing sexual encounter at that, but still…

I couldn't help remembering Sam, the boy, on our graduation night twenty-five years ago. I liked him back then—I really liked him—but, I didn't love him. He was that solid guy, serious about school and his future, just like me. Maybe too much like me. He would have been as loyal and loving as a golden retriever, but I was hooked on a scrappy junkyard dog—Frankie, goddamn, Angelo. Sam stayed by my side as my best friend through all the ups and downs of my relationship with Frankie. It was one of those down moments on graduation night that led me to consider Sam as more than a friend.

That evening was much like tonight—hot and sticky. Was there something about the heat that made us all act crazy that night? Was it a full moon? Or, was it the exhilaration of making our exit from high school and starting our journey to the unknown? Whatever the reason, Frankie, Sam, Marcia, and I were destined for a night that would change all four of our lives forever.

The heat didn't even cross my mind as I took my place on the dance floor wrapped in the arms of my true love, Frankie Angelo. The DJ was playing "Lady in Red" and, as I clung to Frankie in my red and white-flowered sundress, I felt like the moment was ours alone. As the song ended, the boy I had loved so long planted a kiss on me that melted me even further. It was a night to celebrate our love and my final promise to him. I had finally given myself to him the night before—I was no longer a virgin. I wanted to shout it from the rafters but kept it to myself as I savored that last kiss. College would be tough without him by my side, but we could do it. We were committed now, and I knew I would marry him the day I graduated from UC Berkeley. That was the plan. Best laid plans...

The music ended but I wasn't ready to let go, my arms still wrapped around Frankie's neck, my head resting on his white linen shirt partly unbuttoned to expose his dark, olive skin. I knew that skin would be pressed against my newly awakened body in only a few hours and now that we'd opened the door to physical pleasure, I was ready for round two. I whispered in his ear, "I love you, Frankie."

"Back at ya, kiddo." He'd told me he loved me the previous night. Was I wrong to expect those three little words every day? We'd just made love the night before and "back at ya" were not the three words I had in mind. Frankie moved his hand to my ass and gave it a squeeze then told me to keep it warm till he got back.

That was apparently his way of showing his love.

I knew he was sneaking out for a beer and a smoke. It was so hot, I was even tempted by the beer, but I was still a little too afraid to risk coming home with alcohol on my breath, so I let him go and crossed the gym to refill my cup with the fruity mixture they called punch. The heat sucked the moisture from my tongue and dropped beads of sweat on my upper lip. More punch would surely quench my thirst and hydrate my sweaty body. It didn't work—I was getting light-headed and nauseous. I continued to blame my altered state of mind and body on the heat, unaware some of the boys had poured a fair amount of vodka into the punch. Sam noticed me swaying and came over to rescue me. More talkative than normal, we were laughing about the silliest things. With each glass of punch, the giggles escalated. Then it occurred to me that Frankie had been gone quite a while. He could have smoked a pack of cigarettes and drank a case of beer by now. So, I said goodbye to Sam and went looking for my man.

Oh, how I wish I hadn't found him. I'd almost aborted my search when I heard a familiar laugh coming from the custodian's closet. Marcia Jensen had a very distinctive, seductive laugh. I opened the door and found my boyfriend leaning against the wall, slipping and swaying as his legs gave in to the alcohol, his mane of thick, black hair in the cat-like grip of the girl who would stop at nothing to lure Frankie away from me. My eyes moved to the lipstick smudge on the white linen shirt I'd so recently felt against my cheek, the fabric soft and the smell of his sweat-tainted musk cologne still in my mind. The lipstick was not my color and as I compared the shade to Marcia's pouty lips, I turned and walked away. Frankie called to me, his slurred words sounding something like, "It's not what you think, kiddo." But really, how could it be otherwise? Despite his words, he didn't seem to be able to move his drunk ass out of the closet to come after me. What a fool I'd been. When it came to Frankie, would I ever learn? He always seemed to find a way to sabotage our happiness.

Sam was still standing, or maybe swaying, by the punchbowl with a silly grin on his face when I walked back into the gym. I grabbed his hand and asked him to take me home. The DJ had appropriately chosen a U2 song—"With or Without You"—and I planned to take those lyrics seriously. I could live without Frankie Angelo. But it wasn't quite that simple and as the agony of Frankie's betrayal sank in, I knew I wasn't ready to be alone. I barely remember asking Sam to drive us to the beach, so we could get some fresh air. Maybe it was time I woke up and paid attention to someone who really cared for me.

We shouldn't have been driving, but neither of us realized our giddy light-headedness was the result of Vodka-spiked punch. Somehow, we made it safely. Sam stepped out of his Dad's old Chevy Camaro and walked around to my side. It wasn't that I was waiting for him to be a gentleman and open my door; I wasn't the least bit interested in getting out. Sam pulled me up, but I wobbled and fell against his chest. The clean, fresh smell of Old Spice fit Sam to a tee, and mixed with the salty sea air, I couldn't resist the temptation to give Sam a kiss. He was my savior after all—the boy who had been trying to save me from my tumultuous relationship with Frankie for more than three years.

That night, I decided to let him save me. I pulled the passenger seat forward and pushed Sam into the back seat of the Camaro.

Sam had always wanted more than a friendship, and that night, I gave him more than he ever expected. I had nothing to lose—I'd already lost my virginity—he was just there at the right time, and I was being selfish. I wanted someone who loved me, and I knew Sam was that someone. I don't think he was sorry I offered myself to him, but clearly, he wanted to know my intentions. "Are you sure you're through with Frankie?" he asked me at least a dozen times before he finally made the move to unzip my dress. His hands were shaking as he unhooked my bra and felt my soft, young breasts. All I remember about the rest of that encounter is that it was hurried and too brief to bring me much relief, but it did bring me a special kind of pleasure. All I wanted was to be held and loved, so it was perfect…for me, anyway.

But in the light of day the next morning, I felt overwhelming guilt. I had a splitting headache, and my only thought was that I'd slept with two guys in two days. I'd spent my whole life planning to save myself for that one special guy—my Cinderella syndrome was alive and well. But now I felt like the ugly stepsister sleeping with any old prince—or frog. Who was I? This was not typical behavior for Jamie Madison, always the good girl. What had I done? The heat may have been to blame or the vodka that found its way into the punch bowl, or just maybe it was Marcia. Maybe all three played a role in changing the course of my life. In my mind, booze or no booze, Marcia tipped the scales. I could have saved Sam a lot of heartache, and maybe

Frankie would have seen the light if alcohol hadn't clouded the lens that placed Marcia in his view.

Sam and I saw each other a few more times that summer, but I couldn't sleep with him again. I blamed the encounter on the Vodka that had been officially discovered by the school authorities. Not what he wanted to hear—I'm sure I made him feel like shit. I felt pretty much like shit myself, but that wasn't the end of my troubles. The shit was about to get a whole lot deeper.

I was pregnant and didn't know who fathered this thing growing inside me. I'd had sex only two times in my life and one of those two encounters created a baby. How proud I was that I took my time and was very careful choosing the right time for my first sexual encounter. Pretty amazing that a sweet, innocent girl like me, who analyzed every decision ad nauseam, could finally make the choice to lose her virginity and have it turn out like this. The confusion I felt after breaking up with Frankie was an emotional nightmare. I didn't cry much the night it happened because I was so mad and maybe just a little drunk, but the tears started flowing the next day and didn't quit for months afterward. Sam was there for me, trying to help me through, but he had his own agenda and his involvement only made things worse. It wasn't his fault that I clung to him and wanted to have sex with him that night. I took full responsibility—so much so that when I found out I was pregnant I didn't tell either one of them. How could I tell them one of them *might* be the father of my unborn child? What a disgusting person I was, sleeping around at seventeen and getting pregnant, no less.

To be honest, those weren't my thoughts at first. I didn't consider myself a disgusting person until my mother arrived at that conclusion and suggested I do the same.

"What will the neighbors think of me raising a daughter who runs off and gets pregnant? How could you do that to our family, Jamie?"

"Our family? Isn't this more about me, Mom? Our family didn't get pregnant, I did. I just want to figure out how I can keep my scholarship and raise this baby at the same time. I was hoping you and Dad could help me." I was pacing the room at that point. I couldn't think of a reasonable solution and that had always been my strong point. I always had a solution to every problem, but not this time.

"I'll tell your father about this, but don't expect any help. You have disgraced our family, and I'm sure he will agree that we will have nothing to do with you if you keep that baby. We might be willing to help you with an abortion." Her eyes bore deep into my soul, but I didn't turn away, my eyes pleading my case.

"I know it's a terrible thing that I've done, but I'm not going to get rid of the baby. I don't care if other girls have abortions, I can't do it."

"Then you should tell one of those boys to be a man and marry you and take care of that baby." Her jaw was so tense, the veins pulsed in her neck.

"I might if I knew whose baby I was carrying. Do you want me to just pick one and lie to the other?" How could I tell either of them without the other wondering if it was his baby?

"Sam would accept you no matter what. He'd take care of you." Mom obviously picked the one she wanted.

"He wants to go to college, and he has to join the Navy to pay his way. He can't support me and a baby if he gives up college."

"I like Sam better," my mother said as a matter of fact. "But Frankie has a good job at the Safeway store. He could support you and you could get a job before and after the baby is born."

"He got that job to save his own money to go to college. He wants to make something of himself. He came from a teenage mother—he doesn't need to repeat the cycle."

Mom looked at me without a lick of compassion in her eyes. "You're going to have to get rid of it. You have no choice. I'll make the appointment tomorrow."

"I won't do it!" I shouted.

Just then, Dad walked in the door. "You won't do what, sweetie?"

"I won't give up my baby. I'm pregnant, Dad, and I don't know if it's Frankie's or Sam's. Pretty dumb, huh? You thought you raised a smart girl, but I had a lapse in judgment, and I got myself in a lot of trouble." I started to cry. With Mom, I always got mad, but with Dad, it felt safe to break down. He would always take care of me.

"Damn it, Jamie. How did this happen? I thought you were my innocent one. I can't say I'm not disappointed. You have a full scholarship to UC Berkeley and now that's not going to happen, is it?"

I could handle Mom getting mad, but Dad's disappointment was hard to swallow. "I'm not going to let that scholarship, go, Dad. There's no rule that says you can't be pregnant in college. I have seven months before this baby comes, and I plan on going to school."

Mom chimed in again. "The hell you will! We will not give you a dime if you insist on having that bastard child. When you leave this house, don't bother coming back." Her hazel eyes were flashing as she delivered the final blow. "And don't you dare tell anyone in this neighborhood what you have done. It will be our secret and we will never speak of this again. Your father and I are done with you."

"Dad? Are you done with me, Dad?" I ran to him and threw my arms around his neck. He hugged me tight. "You won't desert me, will you?"

"Jack, are you going to let Jamie get away with this? She cannot be coddled if she's going to make a fool out of us. We're done with you, Jamie. You have a plane ticket to school—it's non-refundable so I guess we're stuck with that. When you leave on Saturday, don't come back."

Dad pulled his arms back as I searched his eyes. He caught my eye then looked away, but he didn't stop Mom from calling the shots. Was he going to let me go? The answer was yes. His life would be hell if he took my side, and he didn't have the guts to cross Mom—nobody crossed Mom. On one level, I understood, but at that moment I felt so alone, so very alone.

****

I'd been driving on autopilot as those thoughts raced through my mind, but the radio snapped me back to reality with "Eleanor Rigby." It was an all-Beatles oldies night, and as I listened to the words "...all the lonely people, where do they all come from?" I remembered so vividly the loneliness I felt as I headed off to college.

Should I have chosen one of those two boys to share my child and my life? Would it have been easier? When I looked at both Sam and Frankie, I realized that one of them would have had to give up his education to support me and Justin. And the one I chose would have resented me for the rest of his life. I admit it was hard for the first couple of years, but I made it and it got easier with time. Now there would be a new opportunity for one of these two to resent me when I finally told them that one of them was the father of my twenty-four-year-old son, Justin Madison Crandall.

Chapter Six
My Sister Sarah

Sarah was sitting up waiting for me, just like Mom used to do when I was late. She sat on the rust-colored sofa resting her head on a bright yellow, flowered sofa pillow, her lemon silk pajamas and blonde hair completing the sunny color scheme. That was Sarah—everything that could be a shade of yellow…was, from her cookware to her clothing to the walls in every room. She may have overdone it a bit, but it was a nice change from her black years in high school—black clothes, black nails, black hair, and black lipstick. Honestly, she was the one Mom worried about back then, assuming she'd be the one to embarrass the family. But of course, it was sweet innocent, plaid-skirt-wearing Jamie who turned out to be the black sheep. So much for appearances.

It was nice to see Sarah so full of joy after those dark years. I couldn't help but feel a little envious as I watched her with Samson and Delilah, her two cats. The long-haired Samson stretched his body halfway down the couch while Delilah was curled up in a ball on Sarah's lap. Her kids had been gone for a couple years (at least for most of the year during college), so she refilled the empty nest with these stray cats. If David had his way there would be no more, although I knew he'd give in if she found another one in need. She looked up from her cats and gave me the "You're late!" look.

"You must have enjoyed your pre-function. It's midnight, for God's sake. And you look a little messed up. What were you doing, little sister?"

"Nothing I expected to be doing, I'll tell you that much. I got a little carried away with an old friend." I walked over to the mirror in the hallway to see just how bad I looked. "Oh, God, I really do look like hell. My lips are razor burned—I need that man to shave a little closer."

"You and Frankie got together, huh? I was wondering if you might fall back under his spell."

"I won't dispute the magical spell, but it was cast by Sam Bradley."

Sarah's jaw dropped. "You and little Sammy Wonder? I don't believe it—is he still as nerdy as ever?" She reached down and patted Delilah's fluffy head. "I didn't think you were ever really into Sam. Wasn't he just a shoulder to lean on? Although you leaned on something else back then to get you into this paternity mess."

My body collapsed into the soft recliner that matched the yellow floral couch pillows. "I didn't think I was into him either, but God, he looked great tonight. And Jesus, it's been five years since I've been with a man. So, a little wine, a hot, steamy summer night on the beach, and some unbelievable chemistry…and luckily he let me have my way with him." I giggled, still feeling a little giddy and, honestly, a little surprised I'd opened that door. Paul had been my world for seventeen years, and I never imagined I'd let another man in.

"I'm surprised by your choice, but glad that you're back among the living. Sex is an affirmation of life, and you need that, Jamie. If Sam brings your spirit back to life, I'm all for it." Sarah lifted Delilah from her lap so gently she didn't open her eyes, at least not until Samson snarled at her intrusion into his space on the couch. Patting them both, Sarah rose and headed toward the kitchen. When she returned, she was carrying the tools of her trade as a lab technician, tools that would give me the answer to the question I had avoided for so many years. "From what you've told me you have enough of Sam's DNA to float a boat, but what's on your lips—and other places—is contaminated so I can't use that in my lab. Did you get the toothpicks we talked about?"

"I only got one from Frankie." I retrieved the napkin-wrapped toothpick from my purse. "Sam may have changed in appearance, but he was ridiculously anal about avoiding the fatty, bacon-wrapped meatballs. Maybe that's why he kissed me later, so he could taste the delicious bacon without ingesting the fat."

Sarah laughed. "Same old Sam, but that's okay. I only need one sample. If it's not Frankie, it's Sam—simple as that. That is, of course, unless you slept with any other guys that week. And I thought I was the slutty sister in high school."

"No contest there. I'm so glad you found David and settled down. I think he was your savior." And he was, for sure. When she met David, the black faded week by week, and as crazy as her obsession with yellow had become, I loved the sunny, joyful yellow Sarah that David coaxed from her black cocoon.

Sarah smiled. "David's all right if you like tall,

good-looking guys who make you laugh every day and make you look forward to going to bed every night."

"Sorry to keep you from that bed, Sis."

"No problem. I've been there and got back up to wait for you." Did I see her blush?

"Enough of our sex life, tell me about the DNA test. How soon will we know anything?"

Sarah plucked the toothpick from the napkin with her sterile tweezers and placed it in a glass vial. "Let's hope he savored that meatball and left enough saliva on that stick to give me what I need. If there's enough there, I should have an answer for you by Monday. I'll take it into the lab tomorrow to get things started." She put her hand on my shoulder and took a deep breath. "I really shouldn't be doing this without his consent. Do you think you can get him to sign a consent form?"

"I was hoping you could give me the results before I told either of them anything. Once I find out, I'll ask for consent—how's that?"

"As long as Frankie doesn't find out and doesn't object, we should be fine, but I could get in a lot of trouble running this test without consent. Luckily, my boss doesn't check up on me that often."

I reached up and took the hand resting on my shoulder, squeezing it tight. "I don't know how I'll be able to tell either of them they might be the father of my son. No matter which one is Justin's dad, both have every right to be angry that I kept this from them for so long. I totally screwed this up."

"No, you didn't, Jamie. You were young and scared and what could you have said? And with no support from Mom and Dad, you must have felt so lost. I wish I could have done more for you, but I had to sneak around Mom. She'd have killed me if she knew how often we talked."

"She's gone now, so you can do anything you want. I'm sorry I didn't come back for the funeral, but I figured that would only complicate things. It was probably for the best. I would have had a hard time leaving my students before the end of the semester." I thought better of that statement. "Who am I kidding? I wouldn't have come back anyway. I couldn't face all the friends and family—God knows what she told them about me."

"I could fill you in on that, but I don't think you want to know. Let's just say Mom made sure to tell everyone the estrangement wasn't her fault." Sarah plopped back down beside her lazy cats. "I know it was hard for you, but I really envied you at times. You didn't have to deal with her day in and day out. If I'd been smart, I would have moved away long ago, but I wanted to stay close to Dad."

"So did I...I missed him."

"I know he'd like to see you now, Jamie. Don't let your pride get in the way of opening that door. Please go see him while you're here."

I rose from the recliner, kissed Sarah on the top of her bleached-blonde head, and made my way toward the guest room. "I'll think about it. Right now, I need to go to bed. It's been a long, exhausting day. Goodnight, Sarah. See you in the morning."

"Night, Jamie. Sleep tight, Sis."

****

I was so tired I just wanted to crawl into bed, but between the sand and Sam's manly juices, I didn't feel right soiling Sarah's yellow satin sheets. A hot shower would help me find sleep after this day of anticipated fears and unexpected exhilaration. And there was more to fear as the outcome of the paternity test was about to open an old wound, a wound I thought had healed long ago. But covering that festering sore with a Band-Aid had only protected my son from the outside; it would never heal the hurt emanating from inside his heart. He said he didn't care about meeting his biological father, but I knew Justin, and I knew it was time. My desire to avoid the pain was no longer an acceptable excuse to deprive him of his roots.

I wrapped my red silk robe around my sweaty, satisfied body and stepped across the hall where a plush, yellow towel lay waiting on the red, marble vanity—finally, a color other than yellow accenting her décor—and my favorite. Red was vibrant and had always personified my fiery, outspoken nature, in complete opposition to Sarah's joyful, mellow yellow. Sarah went with the flow, and I always seemed to be swimming upstream, navigating each rock and wave with a determination Dad called spunk. But the constant reach for that spunky core to deal with life's problems had about worn me out.

I stepped into the shower and turned the knob to hot, a strange choice after such a sweltering night, but I suddenly felt chilled with the realization that this week would change life as I had known it for twenty-five years. As the hot water erased all traces of Sam from my body, I wished I could clear him from my mind—his kiss caught me so off guard, and the new-found pleasure that resurfaced after five long and lonely years presented a double-edged sword. Every kiss, every caress, every sensation, was welcome in the moment, but the thought of a relationship felt like a betrayal.

And if all this wasn't enough, Sarah had to throw another morsel on my already full plate by reminding me that my father wanted to see me. It would not be easy to see the man who threw me out—while he didn't deliver the exile order, he was an accessory to the crime when he let Mom's decision ride. Damn him anyway. His passive acceptance of her order hurt more than Mom's overt actions ever would.

The truth was, my dad, Jack Madison, was a good guy who fell under the spell of Nancy Sanders, a very unhappy and difficult woman. His love for her overrode his logic, and I got the short end of the stick. Good parents should stick together in matters of child discipline and mine had always found agreement when it came to me and Sarah. But when I look back on it, Mom made the rules and Dad followed her lead. "Don't cross Mom." "Tell your mother you're sorry." "Do what your mother tells you." Those were the phrases I remembered hearing from my father. I understood his loyalty—he took the path of least resistance and covered his ass daily to keep in front of her wrath. He had to sleep with her at night, and who needs that tension at the end of a long day? He worked hard to give us a great life, but his desire for peace with Mom left me out in the cold.

At least I knew where his heart was. On the Saturday I was to leave for Berkeley, he got up very early and came into the room I shared with Sarah who, at twenty, wasn't as anxious to leave the nest as I was. She took advantage of the free rent and financial assistance while she attended classes. It would be an understatement to say her academic record did not match my scholastic achievements—she had the brains, but her more active social life blocked her direct path to a four-year university. On that morning, Sarah was sleeping soundly, I knew because I hadn't slept more than an hour all night, and the soft, purring sound floating from Sarah's bed, gave me an odd feeling of comfort on my last night at home.

Mom always slept late with earplugs and a mask, so Dad felt minimal fear of being caught as he climbed the stairs and entered our room. I felt his weight as he sat on the edge of my bed but couldn't bring myself to turn toward him. He reached down and touched my cheek, prompting me to sit up and try to look at him—I say try because my eyes could barely see through the puffy flesh. And Dad looked pretty beat himself as he pulled me close and wrapped his protective arms around my shivering body.

"I'm so sorry, sweetie. I wish I could convince your mother she's wrong about this." He wiped a tear from my eye, and I noticed his eyes were damp—something I had never seen in my strong, stoic father. Clearing his throat, he handed me an envelope. "Here, hide this in your purse, and open it when you get on the plane." He wrapped his hands around mine, crumpling the envelope like an accordion. "And don't forget to call my Aunt Dorothy when you get there. She lives in Oakland, and believe me, she will understand, and she'll keep your secret—she wasn't exactly a saint in her youth."

"Thanks, Dad. I know you're doing all you can, considering the obstacle you live with. I just don't understand why you stay with her."

"We thought we were doing you kids a favor by

staying together, and now that you're both grown, I can't imagine leaving her. I don't expect you to understand, but you need to know that she had a pretty rough childhood, and while that's no excuse for making yours difficult, it does explain her moralistic decisions." Looking into his brown eyes was like looking in a mirror. I saw the sorrow in those eyes, but I also saw the love, and if there was any doubt, he made it clear. "I love you, Jamie. Please always remember that I truly love you."

"I love you, too, Dad, but I'm really scared right now. I feel so alone." What would I do when I got down there when I wanted to call home? They made it clear they wouldn't take my calls. My stomach fluttered like a flock of butterflies were trying to make their escape. Now I knew where that expression originated. I really felt like I did have butterflies in my stomach.

"I need to get back to bed now. Mom is going with us to the airport, so this is our goodbye. Take good care of yourself. Study hard, and you and your baby will have a good life." He hugged me one last time and I watched him walk back toward the room that held the woman I would never be able to please. He would never please her, either, but he would keep trying.

Other than the silent ride to the airport, that was the last time I saw my Dad. Twenty-five years without hearing one of his silly jokes, listening to his poetry or history lessons at the dinner table, or just watching him with his grandchildren. He had Sarah's two boys to dote on, but he missed out on twenty-four years with my precious Justin. What a waste.

The hot shower was now lukewarm as my thoughts extended my stay in the small cubicle. The sand trickled down the drain along with the remnants of Sam's incredible explosion—washed away with no concrete evidence of our encounter. Would there be another chance to experience his touch and that mind-body connection that held our hearts for a moment in time? Or was it just a fleeting lapse in judgment on my part? Sam was certainly on my mind tonight, but what about Frankie? Was there still something there? We'd been so close as kids—I couldn't dismiss that despite some of the shit he pulled as we got older. But now I was feeling a bit like Scarlett O'Hara as I made the decision to "think about that tomorrow."

The plush, yellow towel felt like velvet against my skin, even the rough, burned flesh on my left arm and thigh. My face no longer bore the blatant reminder of the fire that killed my husband, Paul, but my body reminded me every day. The pain of more skin grafts was more than I wanted to deal with after all the facial surgeries. Now I wondered if these scars would repulse Sam if we ever got together in the light of day.

As I slipped the silky, red nightgown over my head, the exhaustion took hold. The sheets smelled like a summer breeze, and as I snuggled into them, I watched the ceiling fan rotate in a repetitive, hypnotic motion. Sleep should have come easy. Two hours later, with thoughts buzzing through my head like a swarm of angry bees, my body finally won the battle and sleep took me down.

Chapter Seven
Family

Five hours after my head hit the pillow, my eyes popped open. Between the sunray finding my eyeball through the slit in the bedroom curtain and the smell of bacon traveling through the hall and under my door, rising and shining seemed my only option. The growl emerging from my stomach reminded me it had been a while since my last morsel, a fatty cocktail meatball. The calories in those appetizers had quickly dissipated with my beach romp, leaving me in starvation mode. I dressed quickly to get my ass into the kitchen to help Sarah so I could nibble on any stray bacon bits or shredded cheese I knew she would be using in her scrambled eggs. Despite the hunger, I felt better than I'd felt in years—a glass of red wine, sex on the beach, and an in-person conversation with my sister, and I was feeling right at home. Had twenty-five years really passed since I'd been in Seattle? Things had changed, yet I felt a comfort and safety here, not unlike the feeling I had as a child.

"Good morning, Sarah." I reached for a piece of crisp bacon draining on a paper towel on the counter.

Sarah slapped my hand. "Not so fast—breakfast will be ready in ten minutes. And good morning to you but keep your hands to yourself!"

"Aw come on, I'm so hungry." Making a pouty

face, I reached for a strawberry—she didn't stop me. But the bacon would have been so much more satisfying. Helping myself to a cup of steaming coffee, the aroma waking me before the caffeine entered my bloodstream, I walked over to park my butt on the stool overlooking Sarah's domain. My offer to help was refused, as I knew it would be—she knew my cooking skills were no match for hers. "I'll just watch the master at work as my stomach growls at you. Get that husband of yours in here so we can eat."

"I'm right here. I've got the day off for Christ's sake. Can't a guy sleep in around here?" David was tall and good looking, a perfect match for my statuesque sister who towered over me by at least six inches—somehow, she got the long, lean lines of our tall grandfather, while I took after the shortest Grandma. David looked a little like the mad scientist he actually was—research scientist, to be exact—with his full beard and ample head of dark, gray-streaked hair. His green eyes had a look of mischief as he eyed his wife of twenty-four years.

"David, honey, you know we're meeting your brother at the Pike Place Market today. Besides, we need to give Jamie some space. She's seeing Frankie today." David knew the whole story and had never judged me. The truth is, they'd gotten married a little earlier than planned to prevent my nephew, Mark, from being an out of wedlock "bastard." They joked about it, but there was no doubt they would have married anyway. Even Mark got a kick out of it and told everyone who would listen that his parents had to get married because of him.

My son, on the other hand, truly was a bastard—a

child with no father—but if you asked Justin, he would not agree with that label. Paul Crandall, the man who ended my loneliness and gave me seventeen years of happiness, never once made Justin feel he belonged to anyone but him. The seed had been planted by Sam or Frankie, but Paul lovingly and unconditionally took on the responsibility of raising Justin and treating him as his own. God, I missed Paul. He'd know what to do. He wanted me to tell Frankie and Sam from the start and had finally convinced me to take that daunting step five years ago, but the fire put an end to sharing the secret. The fire put an end to peace and harmony and a way of life I thought would never end.

"You don't have to leave on my account. This is a big house. Besides, Frankie's not coming over until one. I'd really enjoy talking to you two for a while."

"We aren't leaving for a couple of hours. Let's just enjoy our breakfast and catch up." Sarah served an incredible breakfast, finally allowing me to taste that crisp bacon along with her fluffy scrambled eggs and blueberry pancakes. My hunger was overwhelming after a night that was not only taxing emotionally, but physically as well.

As it turned out, we didn't need to do that much catching up. Sarah was the one link to my old life, and we had talked at least twice a month since my departure twenty-five years ago. She and David and the boys, Mark and Eric, had traveled to the bay area to visit, so our families had intertwined, giving me the connection I craved. Losing Mom and Dad left a scar that would never heal, but Sarah had come through for me. After years of sibling rivalry, it seemed we would never find a path to friendship or even basic communication, but my tragic circumstance brought us closer than I ever thought possible. She defied Mom and kept in contact with me, guarding my secret from everyone except her immediate family. What an ally, friend, and source of unconditional love. I couldn't have asked for more.

"So, how's Dad? Does he ever ask about me?"

"All the time. He will never forgive himself for letting you go. Do you think you can forgive him?"

"I don't know. I always thought he'd stay in touch with me. He gave me a letter the day I left. He told me he loved me, but in the letter, he made a lot of excuses for Mom—giving me that same old crap about her shitty childhood, like that was a good reason to be a cold-hearted bitch." I was ripping my napkin as I talked. His lack of communication over the years still hurt like a knife to the gut. "But at least he said goodbye to me the morning I left. You slept through the whole tearful parting."

"No, I didn't. I heard every word." Sarah pulled my hand from the shredded napkin and held it tight. "He did love you, but you might be surprised that Mom missed you, too."

"I don't believe that. If she missed me so much, why didn't she call me?"

"Because you know Mom would never admit to anyone that she was wrong. She never said she was wrong, but she often asked me if you were okay. She kept her unemotional tone, but I know she wouldn't have asked if she didn't feel some remorse." Sarah brushed a tear from her eye—a tear for Mom? "I know Mom was a controlling, mean-spirited woman most of her life, but I can't help feeling sorry for her. She missed out on so many wonderful moments with you and your family by holding onto her anger over your one mistake. It was partly anger about your choice to defy her, and I think the rest was fear, fear of what people would think."

"My choice to do the opposite of what she demanded saved Justin's life. I will never be sorry for letting him live. And now, as a mother myself, I can't imagine anything he would do that would cause me to reject him. I know how crappy that feels." Thank God I hadn't put on my eye makeup because the tears were forming in my eyes now. "Damn it! I didn't want to talk about this. I let this go a long time ago. I had to, or I wouldn't have been able to move on with my life."

David had been quiet during our conversation, which was unusual for him, but he finally spoke. "Jamie, you've done a great job of letting go of the past. You made a life for yourself and Justin in California. Sarah and I have talked about this many times, and we're very proud of you—a little envious, too. Once you left, you didn't have to answer to your mom. Sarah never got to cut that cord until the day Nancy died." He stood up, walked behind Sarah's chair, and wrapped his arms around her neck. "Sarah, I have to say that *not* being rejected by your mother might have been just as hard as Jamie's path."

She turned her head and he bent down and kissed her. "Oh, honey, it wasn't that bad. She was a tough old bird, but living with her couldn't have been half as bad as not having a mother. Jamie may have been free from her constant criticism and bitterness, but no one can feel good about losing their mother." Sarah had such a great outlook on life and never let Mom get her down. She'd certainly been mad at her time and again, but she

66

always let her off the hook. She had a forgiving heart, but I'm not sure Mom deserved it. Although I believed life with Mom had been a difficult road, I think Sarah was right that it was harder for me to suffer her rejection. Sarah's life had been full of annoyances and drama from that woman, but she had not been thrown to the wolves like I had.

"We both had a rough road, Sarah, but at least you had Dad."

"That's true. I'm so thankful for having him in my life every day. Now we just have to get him back in your life."

"I promise I'll go see him this evening. I don't plan on spending too much time with Frankie. I don't want to get back on that roller coaster again." I leaned back in my chair and took the last sip of my coffee. "Besides, I owe Dad something for sending me money for the first couple of years, usually $100 a month—it kept Justin and me alive in those early years."

"Wow, I didn't know about that. A hundred bucks would have been a lot for them back then, but they might have had a little extra when Mom went back to work. She wanted a little extra spending money so they could go out more often." Sarah stood and looked up at her husband. "They were also helping me with my college tuition. If it weren't for them, I never would have met David." She kissed her man and then gave him a squeeze I wasn't supposed to see.

"Will I get to see my grandfather?" Justin had walked into the room while we were talking. I wondered how much he'd heard.

"Do you want to meet him?" I asked as I stood up and gave him a hug.

"I really do. From everything you've told me, he sounds like a good guy. Besides, you're always telling me I do things that remind you of him. I'd like to see where I got some of these crazy genes."

"You got his good genes—intelligence, a great sense of humor, and patience. Hopefully, you'll never need as much patience as he needed with your grandmother." I still had my arm around him. "I'll make sure you meet your grandpa while we're here, but not today. I need to talk to him alone first."

"Thanks, Mom." He kissed my cheek, and I noticed a strong scent of body wash and some great smelling aftershave—although he hadn't actually shaved. The stubble was his style, and with his unruly crop of dark brown hair, I could see why the girls found him attractive.

I sat back down and patted the kitchen chair, encouraging him to park his freshly showered body on the yellow and black, striped cushion. "Sit down, kid. Have some of your Aunt Sarah's blueberry pancakes."

"Can't, Mom, I have a date to go to the zoo. Annie's picking me up, and I think I just heard her car." He grabbed a piece of bacon as he ran to the window. "Yep, that's her out there. Let's save the introductions till later." He ran to the door looking so damn cute in his khaki shorts and orange San Francisco Giants T-shirt.

God, I felt proud of the boy I'd raised—handsome, educated, and kind. He looked so happy, I could only hope he was on the road to finding that special woman who would give him the love he'd been missing.

I turned back to my sister and caught her kissing her husband. They never seemed to tire of one another.

"Hey, you two get a room! I'll do the dishes and you two can get ready for your trip to the Market…or whatever."

They left the room, and I did the dishes, feeling good about being back home. After cleaning up, I went to the guest room to get ready.

A half hour later, I heard the door shut as David and Sarah headed for the Puget Sound Waterfront to explore the Pike Place Market. Memories of the fishmongers, tossing salmon wrapped in white butcher paper across the counter into my mother's waiting arms reminded me that Mom hadn't always been so cold. I could still hear her laughter as she caught the smelly fish that would be our evening's dinner, lobbing it over my head to Sarah as I jumped as high as I could. The rest of that day was full of stolen strawberries, cherries, and raspberries—I could almost taste them. Inhaling deeply, my mind conjured the aroma of fruit mixed with the sweat of the old farmers who came to share their crops. I envied Sarah, not only today, but for all the days she and Mom and Dad had enjoyed the market over the past twenty-five years. Soon I would go back, but not today.

As much as I would have enjoyed that trip, it was nice to have the house to myself for a few hours before Frankie arrived. I was regretting my acceptance of his invitation after my encounter with Sam—I wanted to revel in that connection a little longer and maybe even take advantage of the empty house and soft, yellow, satin sheets. This could not be anything permanent, but I was already a bit spoiled by the reintroduction of human touch and wondered if I could go back to my life of celibacy.

Chapter Eight
Frankie

Steam rose in the small bathroom as I slid into the bath—one last chance to relax before I faced another day of uncertainties. I wasn't prepared for the feelings that surfaced the previous night. I'd wondered if the old chemistry that had drawn me to Frankie thirty years ago would draw me in and, damn it, I still felt a rush of adrenaline in his presence. Sam, on the other hand, was totally unexpected, but the attraction was undeniable. So, why did I feel guilty about these thoughts and actions? Why had my thoughts turned to Paul? He'd been gone five years, yet I felt like I was cheating on him to even think of another man. My love for him was so strong and his loss so devastating, I was sure this day would never come—there would be no more lovers in my life, or so I thought as little as a week ago. But I had survived the fire and was still very much alive, as I was so joyfully reminded last night. So why was I afraid to start living again? And why had I chosen Sam over Frankie? Did I have to make a choice, or could this be a week of reunions with no strings attached? Easier said than done, but I certainly did not want to commit to anything after all these years.

The tub was enclosed on all sides with only a skylight above me to offer a window to the world. I felt safe lingering in the warm, vanilla-scented water until I finally felt relaxed enough to emerge from the comfort of my watery womb. As I stepped out, the full-length mirror caught me by surprise. My body was slim and well-formed, but the wrinkled, red scars marking my thigh and arm reminded me why I could not pursue any kind of permanent relationship. The tryst on the dark beach kept the scars hidden, but no man would want to look at me in the light of day. I was only fooling myself to think either of these guys would give me a second glance without the benefit of clothing. So, I decided to take that benefit to the max as I covered the red, wrinkled skin with tight, white skinny jeans and a formfitting, red T-shirt with sleeves just long enough to cover the affected skin. I blew my dark brown hair into loose, wavy curls framing my new scar-free face in a way that even I found attractive. With my makeup carefully smoothing the remnants of my scars, I walked to the kitchen to make myself a cup of tea. Frankie would be here in less than an hour.

The teakettle whistled as the doorbell rang. It was only twelve thirty—why was he so early? The stove got my attention first, and as I pulled the kettle from the burner, the doorbell rang again.

"I'm coming!" I yelled as I quickly flipped the knob on the stove and ran down the hall to open the door.

"Hi, kiddo." That voice and those big brown eyes… And then he grabbed me and hugged what little air I had left after running to the door, right out of me.

"Hi, Frankie," I gasped. "You're early."

"I hope you don't mind. I just wanted to make sure I had a little more time with you. I still can't believe you're here." He kept his hands on my shoulders and his eyes captured mine without a blink. I returned his gaze until my heart reached the number of beats that exceeded the limit for my personal comfort. I couldn't look at him without feeling the emotions that got me into this mess in the first place.

"So, where are we going?" I asked.

"I told you last night that I'd take you back to the old neighborhood. I'm staying at my old house while Aunt Betty and Ollie are traveling. I may end up there permanently when Marcia and I finalize our divorce."

"I'd love to see the old neighborhood. I haven't been there in years." My Dad still lived in our old house, but Sarah had moved farther north, so even though I was back in Seattle, I had not yet had an occasion to see my old stomping grounds.

"My car is outside. I don't mean to rush you, but if you're ready, let's get going." I grabbed my purse and followed Frankie out the front door.

"Oh...my...God!" I couldn't believe my eyes. "You still have your '67 Chevy Convertible." It was a deep red and looked exactly as it had in 1990 when I took my last ride in "Cherry, Cherry," a name we had given it in honor of Aunt Betty's love for Neil Diamond. Frankie used the name to tease me since my cherry remained intact all through high school—until the night before graduation. It was in this very car that my virginity was finally and willingly given to Frankie Angelo.

"I couldn't part with 'Cherry, Cherry.' I don't drive her much anymore, but I love to take her out for a spin now and then." He grabbed my hand, and we ran to the car. Unlike the old days, he opened the passenger door for me, and I slid my butt to the middle of the bench seat. Old habits die hard, but it felt right to sit close to Frankie again. He patted my thigh—as he had all those years ago—then he put the car in gear, and we were off.

We were on our way back to the carefree days of adolescence. But if we were totally honest, they hadn't been that carefree. Frankie lived with his Great Aunt Betty and struggled with the painful knowledge that his parents had abandoned him. If it weren't for Aunt Betty, Frankie would have either died at the hands of his abusive father or turned to crime himself—Betty Angelo gave him a home and the love he lacked in the first six years of his life. And Frankie knocked her previously reclusive life as an old-maid schoolteacher right off its carefully planned path. I don't know who needed the other more, but together, they forged a nice life—Frankie did not end up in juvenile detention or jail and Betty found the love of her life only two blocks from the neighborhood at the little store up the hill owned by Oliver Vanetti. It was nice to know Betty and Ollie were still together.

During those years, while Aunt Betty and I tried to tame him, he encouraged me to take a walk on the wild side. With my Mom trying to control my every move, he offered me the chance to say "No, I am not going to follow that straight and narrow path." I guess he taught me a little too well, leading me to step outside of that carefully planned course far enough to be banned from the neighborhood forever—or, at least until this moment.

"Jamie, I never thought I'd see you again. I've always regretted the way things ended, so today I'm going to remind you—and me—how much fun we used to have. Life wasn't always such a pile of crap, was it, kiddo?"

"You still have a way with words. No, it wasn't all crap. We had some good times, especially in middle school. I rescued you from a life of crime and you rescued me from a life of rules and control. We were good for each other back then."

Frankie turned slightly, catching me as I stared at the new, yet oh so sexy, laugh lines shaping his eyes. "Let's go back to that time and forget all the lousy turns in between." The deeper wrinkle between his dark eyes told me laughing had not been the source of the premature creases in his olive skin.

"I could use a stress-free hour." With the wind blowing through my hair as "Cherry, Cherry" sped down the road to our old life, I let myself lean into Frankie and breathe.

Frankie talked about his college days and his path to becoming a teacher. He'd done a lot with his life, probably more than he would have if *someone* hadn't led him down a more academic path. I would have liked to take full credit for that, but Aunt Betty did her share.

"So, how is Aunt Betty? I've missed her more than my own Mom—I think she was more of a mother to me than Nancy fucking Madison."

"Whoa! Nice talk. I taught you a little too well. Your Mom was a little controlling, but you sound downright pissed. Shit, she just died, Jamie, what happened?"

"Let's just say she ran me out of town. It was her doing that sent me away, and in case you're wondering, she forbade me to speak to you, or anyone else for that matter."

"For twenty-five years? There's got to be a point

when you quit obeying your mother and tell her to go to hell."

"Don't lecture me, Frankie Angelo. Have you talked to your mother in the last twenty-five years?" Gina Angelo was much nicer than my Mom, but she couldn't break away from Frankie's abusive father, and although she was Joe's primary punching bag, it was just a matter of time before her son would get the same brutal treatment. I hated her for subjecting him to that fear and mental torture in his first six years of life, but I had to thank her for finally having the courage to send him to Seattle to live with her Aunt Betty. If she hadn't given childless Betty the gift of that angry young boy, there's no telling what would have happened to him.

"I did talk to my Mom a few times over the years, but she never could forgive herself for choosing that asshole, Joe, over me. He's my dad, and I use that term loosely, but I can't and won't forgive him for taking my mom's life. Joe didn't pull the trigger, but he led her to the drugs and alcohol that killed her two years ago."

"I'm sorry, Frankie." I didn't know what else to say, so I just took his hand and held it tight as we continued down the road.

He dropped my hand long enough to signal for our final turn, the blinker announcing our arrival to the neighborhood. In the old days, Frankie made his presence known with screeching tires and a burst of speed; now he rounded the corner and drove all too slowly past my childhood home. My dad was in the front yard, watering his geraniums in the window boxes. The sound of the old Chevy caused him to turn as we approached, and he waved. The bloodred Rhododendron bush on the corner of the lot that barely reached my waist when I left home was now as tall as the house. The old rambler displayed nothing special, but Dad's green thumb had turned our yard into an arboretum full of rich textures and colors as vibrant as an artist's palette. I waved back, but did he know it was me, or was he waving at Frankie?

"God, I need to talk to my Dad. I've been so stubborn letting him suffer while I held onto my pain. He must have had plenty of pain himself living with my mother."

"Your Dad's a good guy. He's been great to me over the years. Your Mom was always pretty cold. I know she didn't think I was a good influence on you. Did she blame me for your exit?"

How could I tell him he was the reason, or at least half the reason, my parents disowned me? "My mom definitely had some reservations about you. And she was right that you were a bad influence on me, but you were exactly what I needed to break out of her tight grip." I gave him a wink and hoped he picked up on the playful tone in my next words. "But as she often told me, you wouldn't be an appropriate match for her little girl. After all, you came from a questionable background, and she believed you would hold me back."

"Well, she would have been wrong. You would have made something of yourself with or without me." He stopped the car in front of his old house. The rich, olive green paint was new since my days in the neighborhood.

"And it sounds like you did all right without me. I'm proud of you, Frankie. Except for marrying Marcia, it seems like you made some good decisions in your life." I couldn't resist the dig at Marcia. Would I ever get over that feeling of resentment I held for her?

"She wasn't always so bad. We have a great daughter, and when we were a young family, we had some good times. Now that Elizabeth Ann is through with college and moving away, we don't have much in common." His voice drifted off and I wondered if he was happy or sad about the divorce. "But enough about me, how about you? Have you been married? Any kids?"

"One fantastic son, Justin. And I had a wonderful husband." I took a deep breath and said what I had been thinking. Why couldn't I ever keep my mouth shut? "We had seventeen great years together, so I need to thank you. If you hadn't cheated on me, I never would have met Paul."

Frankie stopped the car in the driveway and as he set the brake, he grabbed my arm, maybe a little tighter than he should have. He looked me in the eye and told me something I never expected to hear. "Jamie, I didn't cheat on you. I had too much to drink, and I let Marcia chase me and even kiss me, but she never caught me—I never slept with her. I thought you knew my big mouth was just a cover—I was just as scared as you were when it came to sex. You were my first, kiddo."

"Really?" If there was any reason to doubt him, I didn't see it. His eyes sought my soul as he shared his heart. He was telling the truth, and I knew it as sure as I knew my heart was about to break. Who was this man? Had I walked away from the love of my life over an innocent flirtation? That damned Marcia! She had plagued me since the seventh grade, and she'd changed the course of our lives with her mean-spirited actions.

Was I overly sensitive, or did she actually thrive on hurting and humiliating me? All because I won the heart of Frankie. She couldn't stand to lose, especially to me.

"Really." He loosened his grip, jumped out of the car, and rushed to the passenger side before I could scoot over to open my door. He reached for my hand, and I gave it without hesitation.

"Let's go," he said as he pulled me toward the backyard. "Who's going to be the first on the rope swing?"

"The rope swing is still here?"

"It hasn't moved in twenty-five years. My daughter always loved coming to Grandma Betty's house not only for the way she and Ollie doted on her, but for a ride on that swing." He smiled that beautiful smile. "It scared me to see her fly out on this thing just as it did our folks. I guess you have to have a kid to understand how our parents felt." It was clear he felt Aunt Betty and her husband Ollie had been better parents than the biological units that claimed the title of his mother and father.

"If my parents were against it, they never said anything. Little did they know how many times we defied death, or at a bare minimum, injury." My folks were surprisingly calm about the rope swing and despite Marcia's parents' effort to tear it down, we continued to soar over that gully until we were seniors in high school. It never got old.

"So, do you want to go double, kiddo?"

"Not a chance. The last time we did that I almost ended up as food for the raccoons." Frankie dared me to go double with him when he first moved to the neighborhood. My desire to break away from my "play by the rules" life led me to the questionable decision of accepting his dare. My mistake was a moment of hesitation—I remember I'd been about to change my mind when Frankie jumped off the bank. I was supposed to jump on his lap, but I found myself hanging onto the rope by my fingernails, legs dangling, knowing I was one sweaty palm away from slipping off the rope, falling hundreds of feet to my certain death. Frankie was only twelve, but he had the strength to pull me in and wrap his arm around me as I scrambled to lock my legs around him. The fear was beyond anything I'd ever known, yet the adrenaline rush pushed me to a high previously unimaginable. This was life—so thrilling when one took a chance and lived fully, yet so tenuous. I would never forget that moment or the boy who presented it to me.

"I dare you," Frankie taunted.

"Not this time. I do want to take a ride, though. I hope I can still do this."

"Just like riding a bike. You can do it."

I grabbed the rope and jumped onto the thick knot that held my forty-two-year-old ass just as sweetly as it had cradled my twelve-year-old butt. I flew off the high cliff, taking the leap of faith that sent me soaring by the giant evergreens above Thorton Creek. Breathing in the aroma of mighty evergreens and sweet wildflowers as the wind played with my hair brought a smile to my face. A smile that erupted into laughter as I tossed my head back and flew out into the blue sky and back to the bank. When all the tension and cares had been exorcised from my body, I jumped off and handed the swing to Frankie.

"Thanks, kiddo." He flashed his signature smile as he took the rope.

Watching him swing out over the creek, I saw the young Frankie flying away from me—always running away from love and happiness. As the rope carried him back, I saw the man he had become—confident and self-assured. He seemed genuinely happy despite his recent marital troubles. As he flew toward me for the second time, he took a leap that sent him stumbling into my arms—it didn't feel like an accident. He grabbed me and planted a kiss on my unsuspecting lips, then pulled back just enough to lock his eyes on mine. Those eyes…

"You look great, Jamie. Has life been good to you?"

"To be honest, the first few years away from home were tough and the last five have been pure hell, but the seventeen in between were amazing. The guy I married was a cross between you and Sam—full of fun and mischief like you, but very responsible and kind of nerdy like Sam."

"I hate it when you compare me to Sam. Shit, Jamie, I hated that you and Sam were such good friends." He loosened his grip on my shoulders. "So, what happened to this perfect guy? You said you had seventeen good years, what happened to change that?"

"A fire," I whispered. "A terrible fire. And I couldn't save him…" I thought I'd cried all the tears a girl could cry for Paul, but I guess they would never stop. "I tried, but I couldn't save him."

Frankie wrapped his arms around me and cradled my head on his shoulder. "I'm so sorry you had to go through that. I wish I'd been a better man at eighteen. If

I could have shown you I loved you, you never would have been there in the first place."

"Did you love me? If you did, why did you kiss Marcia? I know I should forgive you—you didn't cheat—but a kiss meant just as much to me back then. Why did you kiss her?"

"Because I'm a stupid ass, and I had to sabotage a good thing. I never felt I deserved you. You were going off on a full scholarship to Berkeley while I was heading down the street to Community College without a clue what I wanted to be when I grew up. I wasn't sure if I was even capable of growing up."

As I was leaning into my old high school sweetheart, I heard the back door open. A young, attractive girl with long, dark hair, olive skin, and startling, cornflower blue eyes walked out laughing and holding the hand of a handsome young man—my son!

"Hey, Annie!" Frankie yelled, "Come on over here and introduce me to your friend."

"Oh, thank God, that's not your daughter. Your daughter's name is Elizabeth, right?"

"Elizabeth Ann. We named her after Aunt Betty, but she wanted her own identity, so she goes by Annie."

"Oh." My heart was beating fast. My son was dating Frankie's daughter. I had to keep my cool. Oh, my God. Oh, my God. Oh, my God. What was I going to do?

"Are you okay, Jamie? Come on, I want you to meet my daughter and her new boyfriend."

"I know her boyfriend. That's my son."

"That's great! Now I feel better about her dating this guy. If he's your son, he must be all right."

We walked over to the young couple, Frankie

talked first. "Annie, this is my friend Jamie Madison. We went to high school together, and it seems she knows your new friend."

"Really? How do you know Justin, Ms. Madison?"

"You can call me Jamie, but it's Jamie Crandall now. I'm Justin's mom." Did I say it calmly enough? Did she see the sweat beading up on my upper lip? Did she see the fear in my eyes? Maybe not, but Justin did.

"Hi, Mom." He said it slowly and deliberately, not like my Justin. "How do you know Mr. Angelo? Is he your old boyfriend?"

"Well, we dated in high school," I said casually.

"Dated?" Frankie sounded a little pissed. "We went steady for three years—was I just a steady date for you, kiddo? Nice to meet you, Justin." He reached out to shake my son's hand.

Justin looked at me. His eyes burning with questions, but he knew this was not the time or place. He was putting the pieces together, and I knew I had some explaining to do. He reached for Frankie's hand. "Nice to meet you, Mr. Angelo."

Chapter Nine
Justin & Annie

"Nice meeting you, Annie," I said as calmly as I could muster. "Let's go, Frankie, I really need to get back." I waved at the kids, turned, and started heading toward the car.

"You just got here, Jamie. Let's talk to the kids for a few minutes."

"I'm sure they'd rather be alone. Come on, let's go," I said, gritting my teeth so hard my jaw hurt.

Frankie looked at our kids and shook his head. "I guess we're going. I'm sure I'll be seeing a lot more of you, Justin. And by the way, please call me Frankie."

As soon as I was beyond their view, I ran to the car, quickly opened the car door, and settled into the passenger side. I fumbled to fasten the old, antique seat belt, and my shaking hands just couldn't get the thing to hook. "Goddamn piece of shit." My shaking fingers tossed the belt aside, and I put my head in my hands.

"What's going on with you?" Frankie was just getting to the car. "It's not like you to be so short with people. I thought you'd want to get to know my daughter." He got into the car and slid toward me. He put his arm around my shoulder. "Are you okay?"

"Not really, but I don't want Justin to see me like this, so please start this car, and let's get the hell out of here. I'll let you know what's going on when we get out of earshot."

"Okay, but can you come over here and sit by me?"

I slid to the middle. "I'm not sure you're going to want me here when you hear what I have to say."

He started the old car, set us in motion down the road and passed my dad's place once again—a reminder that Justin's father wasn't the only Dad that needed my attention. Could things get any worse?

Once we turned the corner, Frankie spoke, "So, what's your big hurry to get back to Sarah's house? Before the kids arrived, you seemed to be enjoying my company."

"I was. I've always loved spending time with you, damn it. Sometimes I wish I wasn't so drawn to you, Frankie Angelo. Meeting you thirty years ago changed my life; you brought me my highest highs, but now I think we are about to fall to the lowest low."

"Why would you say that? We've grown up. I'm not that rebellious kid anymore. In fact, the timing for us couldn't be better—we have a second chance, that is, if you want a second chance." He reached for my hand. "What could be so bad?"

I held his hand, knowing he would soon want to pull it away. Where should I begin? "How old do you think Justin is?"

"I suppose about twenty-two based on your years of marriage. I can do the math."

"The math has nothing to do with my husband. Justin was born before I met Paul. He's twenty-four years old, born seven months after I moved to Berkeley. Can you do that math?" I squeezed his hand tighter waiting for him to solve this equation.

It didn't take him long. The tires screeched as he

pulled off to the side of the road. "Oh my God. I have another child? What the hell were you thinking by keeping this from me?"

"My Mom didn't want me to have him. She wanted me to have an abortion, and when I said 'No,' she gave me only one choice. She told me I would disgrace the family if I had a bastard child, so I should just go away and cut all ties with my past."

"He wouldn't have been a bastard if you'd told me. I would have married you, kiddo."

"My Mom wasn't keen on that idea, and I was only seventeen, so I needed her permission." How could I tell Frankie the rest of the story? He was always a little jealous of my friendship with Sam and now this. "But even if she or Dad would have let me marry, it's not that simple."

"Why isn't it that simple? Why would you go away and never tell me? I have a son, and I've missed all these years of his life—and all the years I could have spent with you." He ran his hand through his hair, his furrowed brow showing me the level of his distress. "Why did you let your Mom do this to you? Why didn't you tell her to go to hell?" I couldn't look at him and couldn't find any words at that moment. "Answer me, Jamie! Why didn't you fight for us and our son?" He grabbed my shoulders and shook me. "Look at me, Jamie, goddamn it, look at me."

I lifted my head, my tear-stained face finally facing Frankie's glistening brown eyes, his long, black lashes wet with twenty-five years of loss. "I didn't tell you because I didn't know if you were the father of my son."

"What? You've got to be shitting me. I knew you

left the graduation party with Sam, but I never thought you'd sleep with him. I thought you two were just friends."

"We were, but I was so mad at you for kissing Marcia, and one of your stupid buddies spiked the punch and I guess I just didn't think at all that night. Sam was my shoulder to cry on and his comfort led to much more."

"That asshole. He took advantage of you. He was waiting all through high school for me to screw up."

"Don't blame him. I was so pissed at you; I took the lead. He didn't push me into anything. I'm the one that made the mistake."

"I still think he's an asshole. I'm sure he enjoyed the rest of the summer with you. I thought it was innocent, knowing you the way I thought I knew you, but I guess I was wrong."

"You weren't wrong. Without the vodka-laced punch, I realized my mistake and didn't sleep with him again. We just hung out as friends. Then I found out I was pregnant. Shit, I didn't know what to do."

Frankie cupped my face in his hands. "I'm so mad at you for not believing in me, but I guess I didn't give you much to believe in back then. And your Mom made sure I was out of the picture. If she wasn't dead, I'd kill her right now."

I took his hands from my face and held them in my lap. "Between my Mom and your Marcia, we didn't have a chance."

"So, now what do we do, kiddo? We need to figure this out for our kids."

"I assume that means you'll give me permission to compare your DNA to Justin's."

"Absolutely. I don't know how I want this to turn out, though. Having a child with you would be pretty damn cool, but breaking Annie's heart would tear me apart. She's the kid I spent the last twenty-two years raising and her happiness is more important than my own. I never thought I'd say this, but I'm pulling for Sam."

"That would be the best for Justin and Annie, but I have no idea how Sam will react to this news. I wouldn't have said anything to you if it weren't for our kids, and I see no reason to say anything to Sam until we have a definite answer. So, let's just keep this between you and me for now. Sarah is running DNA tests on that toothpick I stole from you last night. We should have an answer on Monday."

"It's going to be a long weekend, kid." He dropped my hands, patted my thigh, put the car in gear, and drove me back to Sarah's house. We were out of words, but I could only imagine his mind was as full of hopes and fears as mine. We both wanted the best for our child—or in his case perhaps children. He might be wishing for two.

Sarah's house was in Shoreline, only five miles north of our old neighborhood, so the silence came to an end long before either of us had made peace with this newfound information or with each other. Was Frankie mad? Was he sad? As the day began, I could have sworn he still loved me, but now he probably hated me for keeping this secret for so many years. Why had I so willingly let my mother send me away, but even worse, why had I let the banishment continue year after year? Even my husband, Paul, thought I should come home and face my mother and Justin's two potential fathers, but the longer I waited, the more I feared the consequences. And now the price of my secret was turning out to be higher than I ever expected.

Frankie parked the car in front of the house. He didn't jump out to open my door this time. He just sat there waiting for me to get out.

"I'm so sorry, Frankie. I should have told you long ago." He sat staring forward as I unfastened my seatbelt and started to slide toward the passenger door. Reaching quickly across the white leather seat, his hand found mine and he jerked me back toward him. His eyes were still wet with tears as he pulled me close and hugged me so tight, my breath refused to escape. As he loosened his grip, the last gulp of air I'd taken in fell out with a sigh—almost a moan. The next few minutes we just held each other, and as his heartbeat kept time with mine, I felt a tear fall on my shoulder.

There was nothing left to say. I lifted my head from his shoulder, touched his wet cheek, and made my exit. My heart was breaking as I stood in the window and watched him drive away.

****

As I sat in Sarah's yellow recliner, the sun found a way to hit me right between my tired, brown eyes. The soft cushion begged me to close my eyes and sleep. The residual scent of bacon and maple syrup still rested in the air, asking me to curl into a ball with a cup of tea. But there would be no rest for me today because I promised Sarah I would go see Dad. She had likely told him I'd be there, so I had no choice but to get back in the car and face another screwed-up relationship on my short, but commanding list of regrets. It was more than anyone should have to bear, but I was tough—isn't that what my parents always told me? "You can do it, Jamie. You're a tough little cookie." They were right, I was mentally strong—I had to be, no thanks to them—and as much as I wanted to be weak and run away, I knew I would live up to my reputation of strength.

So, what the hell…why not just get all the pain over within one day? Who was I kidding, though? I knew this was far from "all the pain," but reuniting with my father was a big piece of the constant ache caused by the secret I'd kept so long.

I headed for the bathroom to splash cold water on my face and touch up my tear-stained makeup. Then, I hit the road.

Chapter Ten
Dad

Sam had apparently enjoyed our encounter last night; the texts had started at eight a.m. and continued throughout the day. Nothing had changed since high school. He still had a crush on me, and now I wondered if I had made the same mistake twice. Sam was always there when I needed him, and I had always taken his gifts, including the package he delivered last night. My body shivered slightly thinking about our encounter but starting a relationship with him was not what I had in mind. Had I taken one more piece of Sam without giving anything back? He gave me so much, and even when I hated him for pushing me to study harder for my SAT's, I knew that without Sam, my scholarship to Berkeley would never have materialized. Yes, he was always there for me, and now that he wanted my attention, I pushed him aside. Today, Sam would once again have to wait.

I sent the text,—*Time for me to face my past. Off to see my Dad. Let's meet at the reunion tomorrow. Jamie*—

Sam's reply—*Are you sure we can't meet sooner? Text me when you're free. Can't wait to see you again...Sam*—

The thought of our beach romp sent heat to that place...that place that had been dormant for five years.

Waking those feelings felt good, but was Sam the one for me? The moment had been right last night, but would I disappoint Sam again? Great sex could make up for a lot, but what I always wanted and always had with both Frankie and Paul, was a strong and decisive man. Neither one of them let me get my way too often, and I liked the challenge and equal footing they provided. Sam challenged me intellectually, but when it came to a partnership, I would likely have to take the lead. I didn't want that.

Stop thinking, Jamie! How many times had I told myself to shut off the brain—quit thinking about the past or planning for the future? At least last night, I had lived in the present, felt the sand on my skin, and smelled the briny saltwater in the air mixed with the musky man-smell of Sam. And today that "seize the day" decision turned my stomach to Jell-O as I pondered my day with Frankie, the guy I thought I would never forgive…and now I wondered if he would forgive me. But those moments had passed—it was time for a moment with my father.

The effort to pull the parking brake to the final position stopped my wandering brain and reminded me that I had reached my destination—my childhood home. Dad was no longer out front, and hopefully, he wasn't looking out the window at me now. Is this what paralysis felt like? Would my legs be able to take those last few steps to the front door? I pulled the keys out of the ignition and waited for sensation to return to my limbs. My eyes settled on the small, freshly painted buttercream rambler in which I had lived somewhat happily for the first seventeen years of my life. Dad had not changed the paint color in twenty-five years, and I could only guess that had been Mom's idea. She didn't like change and, God knows, adding a new life to her family—a grandson—would have been at least as disruptive as changing the paint color on our house. Sometimes it seemed that all the events of her life had the same level of importance—everything was critical. At the time of my banishment, the impending addition of a bastard grandson seemed as important as making sure Dad painted the fence. As I recall, he was painting it the day before I left for Berkeley. I was going to have a baby, and all she cared about was how her home would appear to the neighbors. We wouldn't want to disappoint the neighbors, now would we?

Thoughts of Mom made my blood boil, a churning feeling that still rattled me when I remembered our final parting and the stupid secret pact I so willingly agreed to honor. I hated the knotty, burning sensation invading my gut, but today it served a purpose by thwarting my temporary paralysis as it allowed my legs to function. I opened the car door and set my shaky legs on the uneven pavement. One foot toward the front door and then a quick right turn—I headed up the alley toward the backyard—to the place I spent some of the happiest days of my young life. Days sitting at the picnic table eating Mom's fried chicken and potato salad after a rousing neighborhood battle of croquet on our back lawn. And nights spent sleeping on the patio in a lawn chair contemplating the vastness of the universe as I stared at the stars until my eyes finally betrayed me and succumbed to sleep in the cool summer night. How I wished I could have those days back now. I wanted to walk up to my dad and talk only of those easy summer days so long ago, but that would not happen today. Too much time had passed. The window offering an easy road to forgiveness had closed—maybe forever.

My bare toes peeked out of my summer sandals and turned light ash brown as I kicked the rocks up the dusty dirt alley. Looking down, it seemed as if no time had passed. My feet still looked seventeen, and if only my Dad was still forty-two, we could start this conversation over again. He would tell me my mother was full of shit, and I could raise my dear, sweet son in my own childhood home. But that would be too easy and, honestly, it would have changed the course of my life—and maybe not for the better.

So, I kicked my way up to the back gate, and before I made my presence known by lifting the metal latch, I took in the view. The raspberry bushes were neatly trimmed along the fence to the right, the apple tree to the left of the sidewalk had grown tall, and the dahlias of purple, yellow, pink, and red lined the sidewalk leading to the patio. At the end of the flower-lined walkway in a high-backed patio chair sat my father, his slightly balding head propped in his aging hands. Jack Madison had never looked small when I was a child—he was my dad, my hero, and his 5'9" frame always seemed larger to my young, adoring eyes. Today he looked small—too small and frail for his mere sixty-seven years.

It was time. I lifted the metal latch—I saw his head raise—then I struggled to push the swollen wooden gate past the equally bloated fence post. Dad fixed everything with WD-40, sandpaper, or a hacksaw, but this gate eluded his handy repair efforts year after year. I stubbed my toe, kicking it on the base as I shoved from the top, and it finally swung free. There were so many possible words I could have said to my father after twenty-five years of silence, and I had planned carefully to make sure I opened the conversation in a quiet, respectful way, but instead, I marched down the sidewalk and blurted out:

"When are you going to fix that goddamn gate?"

"Nice talk for a college graduate, Jamie. I see you haven't changed your language."

I could thank Frankie for teaching me to swear, but the truth was, Dad used his fair share of shits, damns, and hells; he just tried to avoid them in my presence. Pathetic since both of us were English majors and should have had more respect for words.

"Sorry, I just wanted this to be easier, and the gate just pissed me off." The frustration of the day made its way to my gut and up to my previously dry eyes. I didn't want to cry, that's for damn sure, but here I was fighting back tears.

"It's okay, sweetie. I'm just glad you agreed to see me. I wouldn't blame you if you gave up on me." His voice was barely audible—such a change from the deep voice that bounced off the kitchen walls each night of my childhood as he recited his nightly poem or prose selection. He was the reason I majored in English and read all those wonderful classics. He was the reason I survived my banishment. Those classics saved my life as I escaped to another world—a world free of my mother's critical eye. How could I give up on the guy who gave me the tools to survive?

"I'll never give up on you, Dad. I'm mad as hell that you didn't find a way to stay in my life, but I know how difficult Mom could be." I knew intellectually that she was the reason he hadn't kept in touch, but my heart still broke knowing he hadn't made much of an effort to contact me behind her back. Loyalty was his strong suit, and he remained loyal to that woman "for better or worse." My assumption leaned toward mostly "for worse." But what about loyalty to his child?

"I tried, Jamie." He kept his eyes downcast. Couldn't he look at me?

"I know, but money wasn't the only thing I needed. Thanks for helping me out, but I needed you, not your money."

"It wasn't much. I wouldn't expect you to thank me for that small amount of money."

"It helped a lot. I wouldn't have made it without the extra money." I could never thank him enough for the money he put in my pocket as I was leaving and the extra hundred dollar bill he sent every month. He risked sending cash through the mail, most likely to avoid a trail to his bank account for Mom to discover. But I would have liked a note or a letter.

He finally lifted his head and looked at me. His jaw quivered but his eyes remained steady as he provided the look that reminded me of the security I felt as a child. Dad was the one who always made me feel safe. "I am so sorry I wasn't there for you, sweetie. I've missed you so much and, believe me, I tried."

"So, why didn't you rock the boat, Dad? Why didn't you rock the goddamn boat? Why did I have to live alone because of that heartless woman?" I had been sitting across from him, but stood up and started pacing, hoping to burn up the negative energy forming a ring around my heart. "I was the rebel of the family, but I guess this mistake was just too big, and I didn't take a stand. I knew she would probably take it out on you.

But you could have done it, Dad. You could have stood up to that bitch."

"I don't blame you for being mad at your mother, but don't call her a bitch. My God, the woman just died. Have some respect."

"Respect? For a woman who would banish her child and never contact her grandchild, just to save face? I'm sure all the relatives think I was the naughty little daughter leaving my family for no reason. What did she tell everyone?"

"She just said we had had a disagreement and you decided to sever ties with the family."

"I love the way she says 'we,' including you in her camp. And you didn't correct her." He was my father, so I resisted the urge to go over and shake him. "I thought I was over this, but I'm mad. I'm so mad at you, Dad, for not standing up for me."

"I tried, Jamie, but she threatened to leave me if I said anything to anyone."

"So why didn't you let her leave?"

"It's not that simple." His voice was soft. "She wasn't always like that. The girl I fell in love with in high school was nothing like the woman your mother became. I always wondered if I had done something to make her change."

"Maybe her rebellious child with the bastard baby made the difference. I just wish you could have convinced her to call off the war and let us come home."

"I couldn't have convinced her. You were always the strong one. I knew you would be okay."

"Did you? How could you know that? Because I had spunk you didn't think I needed as much love?

Why do the sad pathetic bitchy people like Mom get all the attention while self-sufficient people like me are ignored? That's a cop-out, Dad. You sacrificed me— send Jamie off to slaughter and peace will be regained. Can you imagine how hard that was for me at age seventeen?"

"You knew I loved you. I told you the day you left, and I meant it."

"Not enough." The pitch of my voice was higher and louder as the conversation continued. "I needed more reassurance. Just because you didn't get that from her, doesn't mean it's not necessary for human survival. We all need love, and we need to hear the words more than once every twenty-five years." I took a deep breath, quieting my tone. "And oddly, I would have liked to hear those words from her. I always hoped she would reach out to me."

"She was waiting for you to apologize."

"For what? Choosing to have a baby instead of killing it? I may have made a mistake, but did she really expect me to apologize for saving my son's life?" That was the drill in my family. We always apologized to Mom whether we were right or wrong—it was just easier. But the easy way never got my father or my sister, for that matter, any more peace with my mother. She always found another axe to grind.

"That's what we do in this family. It worked for me for over forty years." Dad said the words and I swear he believed them. Letting her have her way was the path of least resistance, but he was wrong. It did not work.

I sat back down and looked him in the eye. "You can't be serious. Every time you backed down, she took the opportunity to find one more fault or problem.

Maybe you should have said 'No, Nancy, I am not going to take your shit! I am not going to let you sever ties with our daughter.' " I reached for his hand and he took it in his grasp, covering it with the other. "I'm sorry your life was difficult, but you had a choice. You didn't have to take that. I know you're mourning her now, but I think you'll be surprised how easy your life will be without her."

"I don't know. It's pretty quiet around here without her."

"That's a good thing." I smiled for the first time this afternoon. "I was alone and very lonely when I moved to Berkeley, but after a while, I found that I was the lucky one in the family because I didn't have to deal with her anymore. Once the shock of her death has passed, I think you'll feel the same."

He smiled, too, a guilty, halting smile. "I hate to admit it, but you're probably right." He reached for a shoebox below his chair. It was old and had once held a pair of my mother's shoes—now, it was held together with yellowed tape and rubber bands. "This box of letters I found in your mother's dresser would have been reason enough for me to leave her. I don't think I can ever forgive her for hiding these letters from me all these years."

"What do you mean?"

"I mean I spent years thinking one thing, and after seeing these letters, I realized everything I believed to be true was completely false. I gave up on you because of her, and I am so sorry, Jamie." The only time I had seen my father cry was the night before I left for college. Now the tears were back, flowing freely down his cheeks through the tracks of his hard-earned wrinkles.

"I'm sorry you couldn't see through her." I felt compassion for my father as he broke down, but I was also angry that he let her persuade him to break off contact with me. "More than anything, I'm hurt that you didn't believe in me. I don't think I can stay here any longer, Dad. I have to leave."

"I wish I could explain what happened." He stood up and handed me the old shoebox. "Maybe you'll understand, and maybe one day you'll even forgive me after you read these letters."

"Well, I know I won't forgive her, but I'm not sure I can forgive you, either. You could have kept in touch with me. What could she have possibly said that would make you give up on me?"

"You don't understand, sweetie. Please read the letters." He put his arm around my shoulder, and I stiffened. The hug I had been craving all these years was no longer desired. He had given up on me without even hearing my side of the story.

"I think I understand enough." There was no way those letters would change my mind, but I took the box anyway. Maybe I would read them later. Or maybe I would just throw them in the trash, go back to California, and forget my Dad for another twenty-five years.

As I walked down the path, I heard my Dad quietly say the words I had been waiting to hear since I was seventeen. "I love you, Jamie." The words came too late. I continued down the walkway to the goddamn sticky gate, pulled it open, slammed it shut, and left my childhood home, this time for good.

Chapter Eleven
Telling Justin

I kicked the dirt and small pebbles down the alley so hard my toes were bleeding. This was my home, the home I had loved for most of the first seventeen years of my life, and even under these circumstances, I'd been looking forward to coming back. For years after leaving, thoughts of curling up in my old, red-flowered comforter on my cozy twin bed talking, or even fighting, with Sarah snuggled in her black, velvet bed cover, made me smile. The smile always grew as I recalled the aroma of Mom's cinnamon rolls floating up the stairs to our expectant young noses. I wanted to crawl back in that bed with a cinnamon roll and a cup of hot chocolate—I craved that feeling—but Dad had just ruined it. Now I didn't ever want to come back.

How could my dad have given up on me? No matter what my mom told him, he had to know I would never have done anything to hurt him—he was the one who hadn't contacted me—there was no way I could write to him without Mom intercepting the correspondence, so what made him think I had rejected him? Somehow, he had been convinced by Mom that I didn't want anything to do with him, but how the hell would she know?

Maybe coming back to Seattle wasn't such a great idea. In only a few short hours, I'd managed to alienate two of the most important men in my past, and I was sure Justin would be next in line to add his name to the list. Sam was the only male still smiling when he thought of me, as evidenced by the text with the smiley face displayed on my phone. How long before he joined the others?

The dust I'd kicked up from the alley found its way into my lungs, and I coughed as I reached the crappy, green rental car. I plowed through my oversized purse, searching for the keys without success. Shit! I kicked the car door, then immediately surveyed the spot to make sure I hadn't breached my rental agreement by denting their precious green machine, but it was clear my bleeding, and soon to be bruised, toe incurred the bulk of the damage. My fingers finally found the damn keys, opened the damn door, sat my sorry ass on the gray polyester seat cover, and started the damn car. Before I hit the gas, I read the text with the smiley face—Sam wanted to know if I would join him for dinner.

My response:—*It's been a rough day. Don't think I'd be much fun. Brunch at your hotel tomorrow at 11:00?*—

In less than a minute, he answered that he would leave me alone tonight, but would be waiting for me in the lobby tomorrow morning. I could almost feel the disappointment in the text—and no smiley face this time.

I promised myself I'd clean up my language tomorrow. Sam used his expletives sparingly and wasn't impressed with my vocabulary during my tumultuous years with Frankie. My calmer years with Paul, along with my position in the English department at UC Berkeley, had been instrumental in changing those bad habits—at least in public. But a well-placed shit or damn seemed necessary at times, and today seemed like one of those times. That being said, I couldn't wait to get the hell out of this goddamn neighborhood and back to Sarah's more welcoming home.

The five-mile drive was hardly enough to calm me down, but when I saw Sarah's car in the driveway, I knew everything would be all right. She had a way of calming me when all seemed lost—she'd had plenty of practice over the years. After the day I'd had, I couldn't wait to enter Sarah's yellow palace, and although it couldn't change the events of the day, a little ray of yellow sunshine couldn't hurt.

"Hey, Jamie, how was your visit with Dad?" Sarah looked at me hopefully as she carved melon balls for the salad she was creating with the fresh fruits and berries from the market.

"Not so good." I raided the bowl grabbing a grape and a watermelon ball. "I can't believe I waited twenty-five years to find out he gave up on me after the first year. Apparently, he was convinced I didn't want him to contact me." My eyes searched Sarah's face. "Do you know where he got that idea? I don't know why I'm asking—of course, it was Mom."

"The truth is, I never had a private moment with Dad until the day Mom died, so I never knew about his communication with you. You know Mom always had to be in the middle of every conversation, so how would I know?" She rolled her hazel eyes, the beautiful eyes she inherited from Mom. The only difference, at least when she wasn't rolling them, was Sarah's eyes were kind. "I thought you told me Dad sent you money every month for the first two years you were down there."

"Yeah, he sent money, cash wrapped in a piece of plain, white paper, no note. I got a birthday card the first year—my eighteenth—and he did write a nice note telling me he loved me and missed me." I ran my fingers through my thick, chestnut brown hair. "But that was it. He told me today that he didn't think I wanted to communicate, so he joined Mom in expelling me from his life."

"Oh, I don't think he ever felt that way."

"Well, he said he was wrong and these letters he found in Mom's dresser made him realize that he never should have withdrawn from me." I deposited the shoebox full of letters on the kitchen counter. "He said if I read them, I'd understand, but what kind of letters would Mom have that would prove he loved me? He removed me from his life, damn it. How can I ever forgive him?"

"Stop it! Bitterness and an unforgiving heart are not your most attractive qualities. It's over now. It's time to grow up. Give the man a chance to explain for God's sake—read the damn letters. Why are you so set on staying mad? I know Dad, and even though you haven't seen him in twenty-five years, you know Dad well enough to know he must have had a reason to do what he did."

"Sarah, I don't give a shit about appearing attractive or even nice. I don't think there's any reason for anyone to reject their child. You have no idea because you've had his love all these years—in person—so, don't lecture me about bitterness."

"Please don't do this, Jamie. It will eat you up."

"It already has."

And there was so much more... A few steps away, a yellow, padded barstool was calling my name. Between the physical exertion of the rope swing and the emotional strain of every other moment of the day, I was exhausted. Sarah saw my pain and produced the right medicine.

"Here you go, Sis." She set a glass in front of me and started pouring red wine. "Say when."

I let it fill beyond the safe level. "Keep pouring. And get another glass for yourself. You might need a glass, too, once I give you the next bit of news."

"What? Did you sleep with Frankie? Are we going to have a repeat of the summer of 1990?" She laughed. "I don't think I can keep sneaking DNA tests into my lab."

I wasn't laughing. "No, I didn't sleep with him, but we had a few tender moments. He has a way of punching me right in the heart. I don't know why he has such a hold on me."

"Okay, I'm only going to say this once, then you can do whatever you want to do." Sarah poured her own glass of wine and took a big swig. "Frankie has grown up and seems to be a good guy, but just be careful. You two always seemed to be at cross purposes and no matter how much you love someone, neither one of you can change your core personality."

"Well, you know what they say—opposites attract."

"That may be true, and that's not all bad—look at David and me—but, it's not that. Your opposite qualities may have helped both of you grow. I think I'm more concerned about the way you two used to bicker and fight over every little thing."

"People change." I wanted to believe that. After all, he could be the father of my child. And if he wasn't Justin's father, there was a good chance he'd become his father-in-law. How would that affect our relationship? "He was pretty understanding today when I told him about the DNA test."

"You told him? I thought you were going to wait until you knew for sure."

"Well, something happened that forced my hand." Now I needed a mouthful of the healing wine. I swallowed hard and closed my eyes. "It seems Justin's new girlfriend is Frankie's daughter."

Sarah let out an audible gasp. "Oh my God! This is terrible." She came around to my side of the counter and wrapped her arms around me, comforting me the way only my sister could. "We better hope Sam is the baby daddy."

"That would be great for Justin, but I don't know how Sam would react. He doesn't like secrets." I remembered my conversation with Sam. "Plus, he always wanted children, and if he found out he had a son and hadn't been allowed to watch him grow up, he'd be furious."

"Oh, I don't know. Sam is so sweet. He would understand."

"There's more to Sam than meets the eye. He obviously cares for me, but I don't know if he'd be able to get past a secret of that magnitude." I smiled thinking of the Sam I had reconnected with last night. "But for two more days, he won't know a thing, and I plan to enjoy the one man who is not mad at me. On Monday, when the DNA tells the tale, I'll deal with the consequences."

As I enjoyed my wine, the smell of salmon grilling on the barbecue invaded my senses. David was in the backyard preparing the fresh Pike Place Market catch as Sarah mashed and whipped garlic into her baby red potatoes. My stomach growled in anticipation as David walked in with the main course.

"Hey girls, what's new?" David asked so innocently, it made me laugh.

Sarah and I looked at one another. We'd covered a lot of ground in the time it took David to cook that fish. Sarah looked at her man. "Sit down, David. Let us fill you in."

We sat down to a wonderful dinner, and Sarah and I filled him in on all the details of my pathetic life.

"This sounds more like a soap opera than your life. It seems the excrement has really hit the fan for you." Leave it to David to find a way to say all that without swearing.

Sarah slapped his thigh playfully. "Oh, David, just say 'shit' already. You don't have to keep it clean for Jamie. She's worse than I am when it comes to cursing."

"Well, then, shit it is." We laughed so hard I felt some of the tension leaving my body. The wine probably didn't hurt, either.

The smile left my face as my son walked through the door. He had no smile for me, and as I stood up to rush to his side, he put his hand out to stop me from moving closer.

"Don't even try to make this better, Mom." The rough texture in his voice told me he'd been crying. He clenched his fists and hung his head, letting out a moan, or was it a sob. "How the hell did this happen? I'm in love with my half-sister—I can't believe Annie and I share the same Dad."

"Not necessarily." I didn't want to tell him about my sexual dalliance so long ago, but I had no choice.

"What does that mean? Frankie was your boyfriend in high school. You always told me the guy who got you pregnant was your boyfriend."

"Well, your father was definitely a friend and of course, he was a boy." I hesitated. "I just don't know which boy."

The color washed from Justin's face. "You're kidding, right?" His eyes searched mine. "Not you, Mom. You always lectured me about making sex something special and you don't even know who my father is?" He rubbed his big, brown eyes, and I wondered if he inherited them from me. Maybe they were Frankie's eyes. But even if Sam was his father, the chance of Justin having brown eyes was high—I remembered my biology—brown genes were stronger than blue. So, I really had no clue who the lucky winner of the DNA test would be.

"I made a mistake. I'm sorry to disappoint you."

"So, how disappointed should I be? How many guys did you sleep with? No wonder you never wanted to introduce me to my father?"

"You knew I couldn't come back. My mother and I made a pact that I wouldn't show my face, and if I found your father, the secret would have been out."

"You should have ended that years ago. Screw Grandma. What did she ever do for you?"

"I don't know. I was so young and scared, and I

believed I was a disgrace to our family. And I couldn't tell your father because I didn't know who he was." I reached for Justin's hand and led him to the couch in the family room. When he stumbled, I leaned in to catch him and noticed he smelled of alcohol. I couldn't blame him, so I didn't mention it as we worked our way to the comfort of the soft cushions. Thank God he'd made it home safely. "But to answer your question, there was only one other guy—my best friend, Sam. I never thought we would be more than friends, but Frankie and I had a big fight on graduation night, and…I turned to Sam for comfort, if you know what I mean."

"God, Mom, how could you do that? I thought you were such a goody-goody girl in high school. And how did you keep this from me and Dad?" He slumped down on the couch—it looked like this day had taken its toll on him.

"Paul knew, and he accepted it. He tried to get me to go home and confront my Mom, and he thought we should find out who your biological father was. I just couldn't do it. It would have caused so much disruption in so many lives. And you didn't seem to have much interest in adding another father to your family."

"You're right, Mom, I was happy with Dad—Paul—I really didn't want anyone else. But since he's been gone, I've thought about finding my roots. And now I think we have to find out. If Frankie isn't my father, Annie and I can keep seeing each other."

"You didn't say anything to her, did you?"

"No, I didn't know what to say. I just told her I needed to go and got the hell out of there so I could think. I've been driving around, stopping at the beach to walk for a while, then I drank a few beers in the car. I was so sure Frankie was my father and, in that moment, I realized I was truly falling in love with Annie." His long dark lashes were damp as tears filled his eyes. "Mom, I believe she's 'the one' and the thought of ending that dream just makes me sick. I hope to God Sam is my father."

"He just might be—he's a science geek like you."

"So, are they willing to give you some DNA?"

"Sam doesn't know anything, yet, but I had to tell Frankie after seeing you and Annie together, so he agreed to the DNA test that Sarah was already running. I was going to do it on the sly and then decide whether to reveal the results, but now I have no choice. You have to know."

Justin's voice had softened as we navigated these murky waters. He put his arm around me and asked, "When will the results be in?"

"Monday morning." I wrapped my arms around him and hugged him as tight as I could. He returned the hug with the same intensity.

My past was not what he expected, but he wasn't ready to pin a scarlet letter on my chest. He knew I was the same kind, loving person who nurtured him and provided him with a good sense of morality—one mistake, no matter how horrendous, would not change who I was. He was very wise for his twenty-four years, and it was clear he would continue to love and respect me regardless of the outcome of the DNA tests. I was just so sorry I was responsible for his pain right now.

"I love you, kiddo."

"I love, you, too, Mom."

Chapter Twelve
Sam Again

I was exhausted, yet I knew sleep would not come easy tonight. After the difficult conversation with Justin, I'd kissed his wet cheek, pushed the lock of dark, chocolate brown hair—that stray piece that always fell on his forehead—off his face. The sadness in his eyes would haunt me tonight. Watching him shuffle down the hallway, head hung low, sent another tear down my cheek. I turned away forcing one foot in front of the other to make my way back to the kitchen where Sarah and David still sat at the table, looking up as I approached.

"Are you okay?" Sarah's voice was soft, and I swore I felt her heart bleeding for me. "Do you want to talk? More wine?"

"No, thanks. I just want to go to bed." I was through talking to everyone except myself. It was time to sift the events of the day through my own personal filter. I headed for the fridge to pour myself a glass of milk—the one beverage that usually helped me sleep—and made my way toward my sunny yellow bedroom.

My mind wrestled with those old heart-wrenching feelings for Frankie, and I couldn't help wondering how my life would have turned out if I'd made up with him on graduation night. Would I have still been pregnant? And if it was his seed that created Justin, how would our lives have played out? I would have had to forego my scholarship to UC Berkeley. If I'd stayed in Seattle, I'd likely be working alongside Frankie at Safeway—neither of us able to afford college. Would we still be bickering and fighting, or would we have found a way to love each other and overcome the insecurities we both brought to the relationship? But if I hadn't gotten pregnant, we would have been free to finish college, grow up a little, and get married. Life would have been perfect. Except for one little thing—there would be no Justin. So, despite the "what ifs" and "might have beens," things probably worked out the way they should have. Imagining a scenario without Justin, even for a moment, conjured tears once again. So, no matter how painful these last few days had been, I realized I would not want to change a thing even if I could.

With the last gulp of milk, those thoughts finally faded to black as I drifted away from reality into a fitful dream world. Dad...Frankie...Sam; the images—both good and bad—floated through my brain all night and even though the clock said I'd slept seven hours, it seemed I'd been awake all night. The alarm signaling my release from those dreams startled me, but I was happy to escape the turmoil of my nightmares to face another day. Of course, there was no guarantee this day would be any better than yesterday—I could only hope, as I always did, that life would get better. Considering all the shitty obstacles I'd faced, I sometimes wondered why I still believed in happy endings.

The smell of coffee lured me to the kitchen to feed my caffeine addiction—the taste proved as satisfying as the aroma. I sat at the counter in a catatonic state absorbing the liquid while I stared out the window.

Soon the caffeine would do its magic, and I'd be ready to start this new day. Sarah and David were off to Costco, according to the note by the coffeepot, and I assumed Justin was with Annie—I had the house to myself.

After a hot shower and an attempt to renovate my tired, tear-damaged face, I slipped into a yellow sundress with a lightweight, white sweater covering my scar, grabbed a bite of Justin's half-eaten waffle, and headed out the door to meet Sam.

****

Sam was waiting as I entered the hotel lobby—I was right on time, but if Sam was anything like he was in high school, he had probably been waiting for at least fifteen minutes. He smiled, not only with his kissable lips but with his bright blue eyes, the laugh lines expressing obvious joy at the sight of me. It was a good feeling to know I had that effect on someone, but a little unnerving as well.

"Hi, good looking. You look great, Jamie."

"You, too, Sam." And he did. The light blue polo shirt matched his eyes, and the khaki shorts showed me just how cute his legs were in the light of day.

"Let's have some brunch." He took my hand and started leading me to the elevator. "I thought we'd order room service."

"Whoa, boy. I know this sounds a little strange after Thursday night, but I don't think it's a good idea to head to your bedroom just yet. Besides I'm too hungry to wait for room service."

"I was hoping to help you work up an appetite." His smile was playful. "Or, was this just a one-night stand?"

"Of course not—that was our second night—there just happened to be twenty-five years in between. But why don't we talk at the hotel restaurant before we go there? I see they have outdoor seating here." I loved that he'd chosen the old Edgewater Hotel—so quaint and such a beautiful, peaceful setting right on Puget Sound.

"Okay, I'll give you a break, but I hope you'll come see my room after brunch."

We moved our conversation to the restaurant, sitting at a glass table on the edge of the pier. The temperature was rising as we sipped champagne and orange juice over our eggs Benedict and fruit plate.

"I'm glad to see you indulging in some fatty food along with your fruit. You wouldn't eat that meatball the other night. I was starting to wonder if you ever did anything wrong."

"I'm far from perfect," Sam said.

"You couldn't prove it by me. You always do the right thing and never get mad. You're almost too perfect, and I don't know if I could ever live up to your expectations."

"Jamie, there is nothing you could do or say that would change the way I feel about you."

"You really don't know me, Sam. A lot has happened in the past twenty-five years. I'm not the same sweet girl you met in seventh grade."

"You will always be that girl to me."

"There might be some things about me you won't like once you get to know me again."

"I can't imagine what you could do to drive me from you. But it seems like maybe you're trying to push me away."

Maybe I was. I removed my sweater revealing the bumpy, red skin branding my left arm starting at my shoulder and traveling halfway to my elbow. It had been painful to use that arm, so it had little muscle tone, although it was coming back with recent physical therapy. In comparison to my right arm, though, it appeared puny and weak. This would show Sam's true colors. "Check this out, Sam. And if that's not bad enough, I've got a big, red, repulsive patch of ugly on my thigh. It was dark on the beach, so you didn't get to see the real me."

He stood up. Maybe I had scared him off. He took two steps to my side of the table, knelt down, and kissed my shoulder. "I don't care about your scars. I felt the one on your thigh the other night, and all I could think of was how horrible that must have been for you." He caressed my thigh so lovingly, sending a chill down my spine.

"Oh, Sam, you're so sweet. I wonder sometimes if you're too nice." He stood up, took my hand, and studied me from his higher viewpoint. It seemed he'd grown six inches since high school.

"Did I seem too nice the other night? I'm not the nerdy straight arrow you knew in high school. I may still be punctual, and I watch my diet, but I also sing karaoke, drive race cars, and I'm an insatiable sex addict when I find the right woman. And I think you're the right woman."

"Really?" My clammy hands made me wonder if I wanted to move forward, but I had to admit, I liked the compliment. I gently pulled my damp hand away and picked up my drink. "I don't know what to say." He had accepted my disfigurement, but could I accept him?

Was he the guy for me? Would he even want to be my guy when the truth came out?

"So, let's get out of here and into that bed upstairs."

It was so tempting. "I can't, Sam. Thursday was great, but I'm not ready to jump into anything permanent right now. I need more time."

He sat back down across from me. "Is time really the problem, or are you putting me in the friend zone again? I know you saw Frankie yesterday. I hope to God you're not thinking of jumping back into that hornet's nest. You know he's no good for you."

"Of course not. I wouldn't go back to that dysfunctional relationship." I hoped I wouldn't, anyway. "But we will always have a bond because of all the shit, I mean stuff, he went through with his parents. He had a rough childhood, and I helped him through that. You were lucky you had such a great home life."

"Looks are deceiving. Frankie may have had it rough in his early years, but his Aunt Betty rescued him, and you did, too. He had a great life up here, but he never appreciated you." He took a deep breath. "Everyone thought my life was perfect. My parents looked like Ward and June Cleaver on the outside, but behind closed doors, my Dad was verbally abusive to me and my brother, and he certainly didn't spare the rod—or more accurately, the belt—when it came to discipline. My Mom took the worst of it, though. He yelled at her for everything and slapped her if she talked back—none of us could talk back without some sort of consequence."

"I'm sorry, Sam, I didn't know."

"No one did. My dad was like your mom and told us to keep our private life to ourselves. We were afraid to tell anyone, but now that Mom finally divorced his sorry ass, I feel a real sense of relief." It was a difficult subject, but he smiled. "So, if I'd told you my dad was a rotten guy, would you have rescued me? Is that how you choose your men—do you need to save them?"

"I sure did when it came to Frankie, but Paul didn't need saving. He was more like you—or like I thought you were. He had a pretty healthy upbringing and a good sense of himself, and he was my savior." As far as Sam knew, Justin was Paul's child, so I didn't go into any more detail. "I guess I'm over that need to rescue someone. So, don't go throwing yourself off the pier in hopes of me saving you."

Sam tipped his chair as if he was going to throw himself off the pier. He grinned when he saw me jump up to save him. "Jamie, you're funny."

"Funny 'ha ha' or funny 'odd'?" I asked.

"A little of both." He laughed his loud, geeky laugh, and I joined in.

"You know me so well." I stood up and grabbed his hand. "It's a fantastic day. The sky is as blue as your eyes, and the sun is as hot as two forty-two-year-olds making out on the beach. Let's go for a walk."

"That would be my second choice." He winked at me with one of those blue eyes, and we were off.

We spent the next hour perusing shops and watching the ferries come and go, talking all the while about old times and sharing some of our memories from the years we were apart. All the cares of yesterday were off my radar for a few hours, so much so that I found myself momentarily forgetting the uncertain future I would face once Monday's news arrived. All I knew was I had been reunited with my best friend—I just wasn't sure if I wanted more.

We ended our date at the top of the Great Wheel, a clone of the London Eye overlooking the city of Seattle. I'd missed this beautiful city and, God, I'd missed Sam. I was happy to soak in the scene in silence, but Sam had to complicate matters. He took my face in his hands, just as he had Thursday night, and kissed me so softly my lips tingled. He deepened the kiss and I melted as he wrapped his arms around me. Maybe I did want more... And then he said it.

"I love you, Jamie."

I hugged him, but I couldn't say the words.

Chapter Thirteen
The Reunion

Sam had not said another word until the Great Wheel brought us safely to the ground and we were well on our way back to the hotel. Of course, he wanted me to tell him I loved him—he'd been hoping to be released from the friend zone since seventh grade. After Thursday night, he had every reason to believe we were beyond that, and although I couldn't say the words, I was sure he knew I cared for him deeply. I just needed to figure out if my reluctance to commit was because I wasn't ready to move on after losing Paul or if Frankie was still tugging at my heart.

As usual, Sam didn't pressure me, and after walking half a block, the awkward silence was replaced by our usual banter. The truth was, neither of us could keep quiet that long—we both loved to talk and always had plenty to say to one another. If I could just keep quiet about Justin's situation for two more days, we'd be fine, but it would be hard to keep a secret from the boy who had been my friend and confidant so long ago. I hated keeping this secret, but I didn't see any point in sharing "maybes."

When we reached my car, he kissed me and made it clear that the invitation to his bed was still open. Maybe after the reunion…

****

Three hours later, I was parking my green vehicle at the Nile Golf and Country Club, the venue for our twenty-five-year high school reunion. I sat in the car and watched several classmates enter the building, wondering if my closest friends—Jody and Jennifer, the three of us better known as the J's—would be happy to see me or mad that I broke ties with them. Either way, facing them would be difficult. What kind of a person did they think I was to leave town and never contact them again? They had both written to me c/o University of California at Berkeley, and I'd gotten their letters, but I couldn't write back—they would ask too many questions and the secret would eventually come out if I kept in contact with them. So, my best friends were sacrificed along with my family. The worst of it was, I let it continue—why hadn't I come back and confronted my mother years ago? Ever since the plane landed four days ago, that question plagued me. Why had I been so afraid of my mother?

My phone startled me with its tritone ding alerting me to a text from Sam. He was running late—damn—it would have been so much more comfortable walking into the reunion on Sam's arm, but it looked like I'd be going in solo.

I stepped out of the car, ran my hand over the skirt of my dress to ease any wrinkles in the black and white striped dress. I pulled it down past mid-thigh. Maybe it was a bit short and perhaps too tight, but at age forty-two I still had the body for it, plus it had sleeves that covered the scar on my arm, so I felt confident as I walked through the open door to the reception table. Julie Thompson, a girl who was an eyelash away from being one of the J's, did a double take.

"Jamie Madison? Is that you?" Julie hadn't been my closest friend, but hung out with me, Jody, and Jennifer occasionally and ran in the same circles. "I saw your nametag but didn't believe it."

"It's me." Julie handed me my nametag. "You look great, Julie? Do you still see Jody and Jen?"

"All the time—they're right around the corner if you want to see them yourself." She smiled a half smile. "Good luck."

The way she said it, I figured I was going to need it. Would my friends ever forgive me for deserting them? It was time to find out. I touched the gold heart locket around my neck—it was my good luck charm with Justin's ninth grade picture inside. For an event like this, I would normally wear something a little brighter and more eye-catching, but I needed my good luck charm tonight. So, I held my hand to my chest as I turned the corner and there they sat. Even after twenty-five years, I would have recognized them without Julie's guidance.

Jody Rose could have been my twin. She was about five feet two inches tall with long, brown hair styled in a bouncy flip—mine had evolved from the flip to a cascade of soft waves—and brown eyes with long, dark lashes and an engaging smile. She was always smiling, and tonight was no exception. She and Jennifer Brown were talking and laughing as they looked around the room observing the toll the years had taken on some of our less resilient classmates. Jen still looked great—all five feet eight inches of her—but different with a short, stylish, blonde-streaked haircut replacing her longer, more unruly, locks of years past. They both looked up as I approached the table and their mouths dropped.

"Jamie Madison!" they said in unison.

"Hi, girls. How have you been?" I tried to keep my voice upbeat and steady, hoping they would do the same. No such luck.

"We've been fine, but *where* have *you* been? As far as we knew, you fell off the face of the earth the day you left for college." Jody's cute smile had turned into a tight-lipped sneer.

"Yeah, we tried to contact you, but never heard a word. And we know you got our letters because they were never returned." Jen had always been rather blunt and didn't smile as freely, so her stern look didn't surprise me. "We were your best friends, Jamie. What the hell happened?"

"It's a long story, and I don't expect you guys to welcome me with open arms after I dropped you from my life, but there really was a reason I couldn't talk to anyone. You weren't the only ones I had to desert."

"So, did you see some horrific crime and have to go into the witness protection program?" Jody asked. "I could forgive you for that, but I can't think of any other reason I might forgive you. We were the J's, Jamie; we were inseparable, and suddenly, you quit speaking to us. What are we supposed to think?"

"Please give me a chance. I can't explain it all now because there are still some things I need to resolve, but suffice it to say, my Mom banished me from all family and friends. She said she would have my scholarship revoked if I spoke to anyone, so I went off to school and never looked back." I pulled a chair from the nearby table and sat it between my two friends. They made room for me and continued to listen. "I wanted to call you, but I was sworn to secrecy and all over something so stupid. You two know my Mom—she was never easy."

"I could see your Mom being a real bitch," Jennifer said, warming up to the possibility that I was a victim of my mother's arbitrary righteousness.

"You didn't want to cross Mrs. Madison, that's for sure," Jody echoed.

"Well, you don't have to worry about that anymore. She died three months ago. That's why I came back. I thought about staying in California, knowing how hard it might be to rekindle old friendships, but I decided to come back and jump into the fire." Did I say that? What a terrible choice of words after what I'd been through.

"I'm sorry about your mom. I'm not sure you'll be welcome back here, but I will say you are very brave to make the effort." Jody's tone was kind.

"I don't know if you can ever forgive me—I wouldn't really blame you if you walked away—but, I know you two, and I believe you'll give me a second chance. I hope so anyway."

Jody reached over and squeezed my hand. "It's going to take some time to put this behind us, but I'm okay with giving you another chance. How about you, Jenny?"

"I don't know," Jennifer said. "It depends on whether you're still interested in Frankie Angelo. I got divorced a couple of years ago, and I hear Frankie's back on the market."

"I never knew you were interested in Frankie." I couldn't believe Jen had never told me.

"I was always envious of your relationship. In fact,

I have a confession." Jen looked at me briefly, then turned away, focusing her eyes on the cocktail napkin on the table in front of her. "When you deserted us, and him apparently, I figured there was no reason to be loyal to our friendship, and when he asked me out, I jumped at the chance."

"Wow. I had no idea. I thought he and Marcia got together as soon as I left. They were all over each other on graduation night. What happened?" My eyes were wide as I searched her face. She finally looked up.

"Marcia dumped him the minute you left town. What was it with you and Marcia, anyway? She only wanted Frankie when you had him."

"I don't think Marcia could stand to lose to me. She made such a point of letting me know I wasn't cool enough for her group of friends, so she took it personally when *the one and only* Frankie Angelo chose me over her." I knew I deserved him, but no one knew our childhood history so, on the surface, it looked like he was out of my league. Well, *almost* no one knew our history—Marcia knew and should have understood our bond, but she just didn't give a damn.

Jen looked at me with her steely gray eyes. "So are you back to reclaim Frankie or not?"

"I wasn't planning on it." And that was true, but...the best-laid plans always seem to go awry. I really didn't know how I felt at this point. "He does look pretty hot over there, though." He was over talking to Gary Daniels, the guy who spiked the graduation punch. "But tell me how he ended up with Marcia."

Jen knew the story—she'd obviously kept in touch with him for a while. "Frankie had just transferred from community college up to Western State University.

Marcia had been up there for two years and was engaged to some guy who looked a lot like Frankie, except for the eyes—this guy apparently had piercing blue eyes. He was an art student like Marcia."

"So why didn't she marry this other guy?"

"He was a little wild. He liked to ride his motorcycle everywhere, rain or shine, and one rainy day he took a sharp turn on Chuckanut Drive faster than his bike could handle. He didn't survive the crash."

"So, she started seeing Frankie after she lost her boyfriend?" I asked.

"Yeah, like immediately after he died. The next thing we hear, she and Frankie were married. It was weird."

Jody chimed in. "You two are both better off without Frankie. I always thought you should have gone for Sam, Jamie."

A deep voice answered. "I totally agree with you, Jody." Sam had walked in and was standing behind me. "I've been trying to tell her that since seventh grade."

I should have sensed his presence. The smell of Old Spice was subtle, but I always felt a rush of adrenaline along with a feeling of comfort when his scent passed my nose. Was it the Old Spice that evoked that response? Or, was it Sam?

There was a great buffet dinner waiting, so the four of us went through the line and spent the next hour talking and savoring the delicious spread—now I knew why they charged us so much for this event. Honestly, hot dogs and beer would have been fine, and it would have allowed more of our classmates to attend, but it only happened every five years, so I guess it was worth it. The price was a bargain if it opened the door to rekindling friendships with Jody and Jennifer—maybe even Julie, who had joined us and seemed to be warming up. Although, I wasn't sure if she was warming up to me or Sam.

I got my answer five minutes later when the music started. The DJ chose a song from our era, "Livin' on a Prayer" by Bon Jovi and while Sam was smiling at me and only me, Julie stood up and walked over to Sam, took his hand, and asked him to dance. Either she didn't see what was happening with us or she didn't care—she was going after what she wanted. Sam looked over his shoulder and gave me a smile and a wink as he let Julie drag him out to the dance floor.

Jody was the only one of us with a happy marriage. She had married a sweet guy she met at the University of Washington, and they'd been married twenty years, so my friendship with her would probably be safe. Julie and Jennifer might be less forgiving when they realized both Frankie and Sam had been pursuing me.

Frankie and Gary Daniels were walking toward our table. I looked at Jen, her eyes wide and welcoming as she smiled at the guys. She seemed to be hoping for a reunion with Frankie. I guess I knew how she felt. I still got a rush when I saw him, and tonight was no exception. Did he remember our graduation party, or was it just a coincidence that he was wearing a creamy, white-linen shirt that accented his dark, olive skin—just like the shirt he wore that night? He glanced at Jennifer, gave her his signature wink, then turned to me.

"May I have this dance, kiddo?" He extended his hand to me.

"Sure." I felt the heat coming from Jen's direction, but when Gary asked her to dance, how could she complain? He was as hot as Frankie ever hoped to be, and if he was second choice, I'm sure Jen would be able to live with that.

Frankie took my hand as we walked to the dance floor and my heart rate immediately increased. Why did he still do this to me? Then, I looked up to see a smiling Sam coming toward us and as his bright blue eyes moved from my face to my hand wrapped in Frankie's grasp, my racing heart skipped a beat. Between the two of them, I wasn't sure my heart would survive. After viewing my attachment to Frankie, Sam's smile faded, he shook his head and turned away. I wanted to run after him, but I also wanted to share this next dance with Frankie. Sam would just have to understand that I was not ready to be claimed quite yet…maybe not ever.

The young DJ decided it was time to slow things down and create some nostalgia for us middle-aged reunion-ites with "Always on my Mind"—a very slow song that would require close contact with Frankie. My free hand touched his shoulder, the heat of his body penetrating the soft, white linen, while the other hand remained lost in Frankie's secure grip.

"I'm surprised you wanted to dance with me after yesterday," I said, hoping he'd tell me everything was all right.

"I'm still pissed as hell that you didn't tell me about your, or maybe *my*, son. But we're in this together now, and we need to figure it out."

"Did you tell Annie? I told Justin, and he was not only heartbroken about how this might affect the two of them, but I feel like he lost respect for me."

"Jamie, you're human. You made a mistake. He's old enough to understand that, and I'm sure he will not love you any less because you slept with Sam. I think I'm the one who's most surprised by that." His hand moved down my spine, and he pulled me closer. "And yes, I told Annie."

"How did she take it?"

"Surprisingly well. Even though it's obvious to me that she loves Justin, she doesn't believe in worrying about something that may not happen. I don't know where she got her patience—it certainly wasn't from me or Marcia."

Despite the tough conversation, I felt safe in Frankie's arms, just as I had twenty-five years ago just before the big blowup. Was I still that naïve young girl or was Frankie ready for a mature relationship? He was the one who was, as the song reminded me, always on my mind—at least for my first year in Berkeley. I moved my hand to his neck and laid my head on his shoulder.

"You feel so good, kiddo. I wish this shit was over, so we could start again."

"So, you're really over Marcia already?"

"Of course. You were right, she really is a pain in the ass. I don't know why I didn't see through her years ago." He leaned back to open some space between us. "But she is Annie's mother, so I told her about the DNA test."

I pushed away further. "Why? Why would you tell her something like that before we even know if you are involved?"

"Force of habit, I guess. We always told each other everything. This seemed important, don't you think?"

"Are you sure you're divorcing? You two act like you're still a couple—a dysfunctional couple, but a couple nonetheless."

Out of the corner of my eye, I noticed Sam was back on the dance floor—with Marcia. She wouldn't have gone near him in high school when he was head of the Science Club, but now that he looked hot and was interested in me, she was all over him.

I looked at Frankie. "What's with Marcia's sudden interest in Sam?"

"Maybe the same as yours. You two seem to have rekindled your *friendship* or whatever you want to call it."

"What do you mean by that?" The distance between our bodies was widening. "I was happy to see Sam, just as I was happy to see you again."

"I saw you two coming back from the beach. You looked pretty damn happy all right. That guy isn't the sweet, dorky guy you would have me believe. He had to be pretty smooth if he talked you into cheating on me in high school?"

Were we fighting again? Would things ever change with us? "Are you jealous, Mr. Angelo? I don't believe I am anyone's property—not yours or Sam's. And he didn't talk me into cheating—your actions with Marcia and your friend's stupid idea to put vodka in the punch pushed me into his arms. Sam had very little to do with that decision—it was my choice."

"Hey, I'm sorry, kiddo. I didn't mean to piss you off. It's just that I miss you, and I don't want Sam to take you away from me."

"I know. I've missed you, too." I leaned back in. This felt like a repeat of an old movie. We would get upset and bicker, then say we were sorry, and all was well again—or was it? Did I want to ride that roller coaster again?

I laid my head back on his shoulder and watched Sam and Marcia with a tinge of jealousy. They were talking as they danced. She was smiling as she obviously shared some cute story, but Sam was not laughing. He was looking at me—definitely, not laughing. As the song ended, he left Marcia standing there and walked deliberately toward me, pulled me from Frankie's arms, and led me off the dance floor and out the door into the parking lot.

"When were you going to tell me?" His blue eyes flickered like the tip of a hot flame. "I might be a father, something I've always wanted, and you never bothered to tell me? And even after all these years, you told Frankie and not me."

"I had to tell Frankie. His daughter is dating my son—we had to keep them apart."

"No excuse. You should have told both of us, and you should have told us years ago." He closed his eyes. "If Justin is my son, I've missed twenty-four years of being a dad." A tear doused the flame in his eyes as he continued. "How could you keep this from us for so long?"

"Remember when I told you I was glad my mom was dead?" He nodded. "Well, as long as she was alive, she made it clear that I was not to tell anyone about my bastard baby. She told me I had shamed the family and threatened to revoke my scholarship if I didn't keep our little secret."

"She couldn't have done that, could she?"

"I don't think so, but I didn't know that then, so I kept quiet until I graduated from college. By then, I'd met my husband, and he had adopted Justin, which was legal since his father was 'unknown'. I kept thinking about coming back, but it just got harder and harder as the years passed."

"Life isn't easy, Jamie. You really screwed this one up. You had no right to keep this from me."

"I thought I was saving you and Frankie from the responsibility of fatherhood." I looked at the ground to avoid his venomous stare. "Now I know I took something precious from one of you. What would your wife have done if you had a child? I worried about that."

"That would have been my problem. You needed to give me the information and let me figure it out from there." He was pacing in front of me, his fist hitting his open palm. "I get that your Mom was a bitch and you bought into the program, but when you grew up, you should have told her to go to hell. You're not the girl I thought you were, Jamie. You're a liar just like my ex-wife."

He was right. I wasn't the perfect girl, the girl he put on a pedestal so many years ago. It was about time he realized that, but I wished I could have shown him with a smaller flaw. My inability to share this secret, to share the truth with the possible father of my child, was a deal breaker. Even if Sam was not the father, the look in his eyes told me he would not forgive me for withholding this information. I'd never seen that look, and as bad as I felt, I had a new respect for Sam. He wasn't just a pushover—he had a strength I couldn't help but admire.

"I didn't actually lie—I just disappeared. I wasn't trying to hurt you." I searched his eyes for some acceptance, but there was not an ounce of forgiveness in his gaze.

"Well, you did a good job without even trying. I don't see us getting past this, but of course, I want to know if Justin is my son. When will you have the results?"

"Monday." My eyes filled with tears. "Are you sure we can't get past this?"

"Looks like you're still into Frankie, so why do you even care? I hope he is the father so I can get out of here and leave you behind."

"You don't mean that, do you?" I pleaded. The gravity of losing Sam was hitting me harder than I expected. I had lived without him for twenty-five years, but now I wasn't sure if I wanted a life without him. I reached for his hand and he pulled it away.

"I mean it, Jamie. I don't want to be runner up to Frankie, and I'm tired of begging you to open your eyes to the love that has been right in front of you. You couldn't see it then and you don't see it now, so you can go to hell."

"But I do see it, Sam. I'm just scared."

"It doesn't matter. It's too late." He turned and walked back inside.

I fell to the ground and sobbed, wishing I'd never come back home.

Chapter Fourteen
The Letters

The reunion was over for me. I lifted my aching head from the fetal position as small pebbles on the hard parking lot surface ground into my knees. What a mess I was, my face sodden with tears and my heart heavy with the loss of Sam. How much more could I take? I stood slowly and walked to my car only to realize my purse with my car keys was still inside. Damn it, the last thing I wanted to do was walk back in there to see Marcia and her clique of bitches pointing and laughing at me. I could only guess the word had spread around the room rather quickly from her circle of gossipmongers. What was I going to do? I leaned against the driver's door and held my head in my hands. And then the only good thing that was going to happen, happened. Jody Rose came out with my purse in her hand.

"Hey, Jamie, you might need this." Jody held up my small, black bag. "Sam said he didn't think you'd be coming back in and asked me to take it to you."

"That was nice of him. I'm surprised he bothered. He's pretty mad at me right now. I'm sure he told you girls all about it."

"Actually, no. He didn't tell us a thing. He just sat there saying 'Damn her!' over and over." Jody looked at my swollen eyes. "What did you do to that man, or better yet, what did he do to you? You both look terrible."

"Oh, Jody, I promise I'll tell you all about it next week. I just want to go home now." I hugged her and she held me tight. If anyone would forgive me for twenty-five years of silence, she would be the one. "Thanks for saving me the humiliation of going back in there. If you want to know what's going on, just ask Marcia."

"I'll wait for you to tell me. I have no interest in talking to Marcia." She squeezed my hand. "Just go home and take care of yourself. We'll talk soon."

Taking a deep breath and releasing a sigh of relief, I pulled the key from my purse, unlocked the car door, and prepared to escape from this nightmare. I took my place in the driver's seat of the green machine and pushed the limits of her speedometer all the way to Sarah's house. As I pulled into the driveway, I was, indeed, relieved to have escaped the reunion, but the nightmare had followed me home.

The tritone ding alerting me to a text sent my heart racing. Was Sam going to forgive me after all? My hand trembled as I reached for the phone; I pulled it out slowly as if I could will the right words onto the screen. And there it was: a text from Frankie.

Frankie: —*Where did you go, kiddo?*—

Where the hell did he think I went? His big mouth had caused so much trouble, and he was clueless. Or, maybe he was glad that Marcia created the rift between Sam and me. Was that his plan? I didn't know and I wasn't in the mood to discuss it with him, but I answered.

Me: —*I had to leave. Marcia told Sam our secret.*

Why did you tell her?—

Frankie: *—He would have found out Monday, anyway. What's the big deal?—*

Me: *—You really don't get it, do you?—*

Frankie: *—I just want to see you. Can I come over later?—*

Me: *—No. I don't want to talk right now. Tell Marcia to duck off!—* That wasn't what I meant to say. I sent one last text. *—Damn autocorrect!—*

Frankie got the message and left me alone—so alone. Two days ago, I wondered if there was still a spark between us. There was. But was the feeling in my gut tonight a prediction of trouble? Dad always told me I would know I was in love if I felt butterflies in my stomach, but the buzzing in my belly tonight seemed more like angry hornets. Frankie and I never were a normal couple, maybe hornets were our more intense manifestation of that old butterfly cliché. No matter, though, I did not want to deal with him tonight.

And Sam… My heart ached as my mind replayed his rejection. This morning he loved me, and tonight, he hated me. And with Sam there was no chance for redemption—good old "black and white" Sam had made up his mind, so even if I did want more than friendship, he would probably not give me a second chance.

So, it was time to go back to my original plan— find Justin's father then get the hell back to Berkeley. These past few days made me realize that even though my husband had died, I was not dead yet and deserved to find love, but it didn't look like I would find it here. I was mad at Frankie and Sam was mad at me, so I was back to nothing, no one.

That wasn't quite true. I had my sister, and I had Justin—at least for the moment. Would he turn away from me if Frankie was his father? That would change the course of his life.

****

The one person I wanted to see after my horrible ordeal was my sister, and when I walked in the door, there she was, sitting on the couch reading a stack of letters—the letters Dad had given me yesterday. She and David had their reading glasses on, each holding one side of the same letter as they sat so close you couldn't slip a sheet of paper between them. They could have divided the task of reading the letters, but they chose to share each word as they shared almost everything in their life. Seeing the two of them felt like looking in the mirror of my life with Paul. We, too, had that desire to be connected; there seemed to be an invisible thread that held us together, tugging at my heart when we were apart for more than a few hours.

I should have been happy to see Sarah still enjoying what I had lost, but I felt so empty right now, and just looking at them sent waves of envy through me.

"So, did you solve the mystery of the letters?" My tone was accusing rather than inquisitive. I didn't think anything could change my feelings for my dad, knowing he had chosen not to communicate with me all those years. But even that was no excuse for the sarcastic nuance in my voice.

"Are you all right, Jamie?" Sarah asked as she looked up over the top of her reading glasses. "You're home awfully early."

"Things didn't go well. Marcia hasn't changed a

bit, and she decided to share my little secret with Sam. Needless to say, Sam wasn't happy, and he pretty much told me to go to hell." The sarcasm continued as I said, "Other than that, it was a lovely evening."

Sarah heard the nasty tone of my voice, but she let it go. "Come here, Jamie. Come sit with us."

I moved toward the couch, still resenting their happiness a bit, but when I got there and Sarah hugged me tight, my envy turned to gratitude. I was so happy to have both her and David in my life. The tears I thought I'd left in the parking lot returned as I laid my head on her shoulder.

David reached over and squeezed my hand. "We're here for you, Jamie. We'll help you through this."

"Thanks, you two." I sat up and separated myself from them. "So, tell me what these letters are all about. What was Mom keeping in her dresser drawer all these years?"

"You might want to brace yourself, Sis. Do you want a glass of wine before we tell you what's going on?"

"No, I think wine would just make me sick. Maybe I'll make myself some tea." Needing a few minutes to prepare for whatever the news might be, I stood up and headed for the kitchen to put the kettle on. It was still hot outside, but the chill I felt so deep inside needed a warm, soothing cup of something. As I sat on the barstool waiting for the kettle to whistle, I couldn't help wondering what could be in those letters. They were in Mom's dresser drawer, so who was she communicating with? And how would they ever justify my dad's decision to reject his little girl all those years ago?

The whistle brought me back to reality, and I

prepared the fragrant orange spice tea and headed back to the living room. The yellow, floral recliner was more than inviting after the events of a day that started out beautifully, rose to the height of the Great Wheel, and then plummeted to the hard pavement. Whatever the letters had to offer, I could take it. There was nothing more that could hurt me at this point—I was already at the bottom.

Sarah could see I was beat, so she started very gently. "Jamie, I don't want you to think any less of Mom, but she sabotaged Dad's attempt to contact you."

"How could I think any less of Mom? She stole twenty-five years of my life from me. But what does that have to do with Dad?"

"These letters aren't to or from Mom." Sarah had a tear in her eye. "These letters are from Dad, addressed to you. Dad took them to the mailbox, but once he went to work, Mom retrieved them and made sure they never got to you. And they were all opened so she read every one."

"How do you know Dad actually took them to the mailbox?" I asked.

"I called him about halfway through reading them. He confirmed that he put every one of them in the mail. He also said he mailed the first letter and a birthday card from his office."

"That explains why I got those. He must have sent the money from his office, too."

"Maybe. He didn't say anything about that." Sarah had an inquisitive look on her face. "I wonder why he didn't mention the money."

"He probably didn't want to make a big deal of it. Dad was never one to ask for praise." The feeling of pure joy caught on a lump in my throat. "Oh my God, Sarah. He did love me. He really did love me." But after the joy, the anger made its way to my tongue. "And Mom screwed me over again and again and again. It's a good thing she's dead because it saves me from committing murder. How could she do this to me?"

"She didn't want any competition. You took the attention away from her, so she made Dad think you were the one ending the communication. She told him you were selfish and ungrateful if you couldn't even answer his letters…and he believed her."

"And *I* believed he rejected me. I guess we were both fooled." I drank from the hot cup of tea; the chill was lifting. "I guess I owe Dad an apology. Do you think it's too late to call?"

"Why don't you just wait until tomorrow? I invited him to an early Sunday dinner." Sarah smiled. "For now, just sit back and read some of these wonderful letters. Dad always did have a way with words, and he had some beautiful ones for you." Her eyes glossed over with tears. "He loves you, Jamie. And I love you, too, Sis."

I jumped out of the recliner and took a leap toward the couch. I reached out for my sister, the only person who seemed to understand how I was feeling, and grabbed her in the tightest hug I could muster. "I love you, Sarah. Thanks for giving me back my Dad…*our* Dad. How can I ever thank you?"

"What about me?" David piped up. "I read the letters, too. I knew Dad wouldn't have sold you down the river unless there was some extenuating circumstance."

I reached across Sarah and squeezed his hand.

"Thank you, David. It was our lucky day when you walked into Sarah's life." And it was. I loved David as if he was my own brother, and I'm sure Dad was happy to have such a wonderful son-in-law. It was just such a shame that Paul couldn't have shared that spotlight, and I had to admit, I was a little resentful. "You've had more years with Dad than I have. You know him better than I do." I felt a wistful longing as I said the words.

Those twenty-five years were gone, but tomorrow I would have a chance to open the door to the next twenty-five. Feeling the flutter of nerves in my gut as I plopped back down in the recliner reminded me of how I'd treated Dad yesterday. I must have hurt him deeply. I could not wait to make it up to him and introduce him to his oldest grandson. Justin was going to love his grandpa.

The key turned in the front door and in walked my sweet Justin. "Hi, Mom!" he said in a voice a little too cheery for our circumstances.

"You're awfully cheery," Sarah said. "I hope you checked your blood alcohol before driving."

"I had one beer, but that's not why I'm happy." He came over to the recliner and leaned down to hug me. "I just have a good feeling that Frankie is not my Dad. Annie and I have been talking and I am nothing like him. I think I'm more like your friend Sam—a total nerd."

"You could have gotten that from Paul," I said. "It's not always in the genes. You lived with a science professor for seventeen years."

"Well, I am a lot taller than Frankie at five feet eleven inches to his five feet nine inches, and I don't have his dark skin."

"That's because you look exactly like me and you could have gotten your height from your grandmother's side of the family." I took his hand in mine. "I don't want to burst your bubble, but this isn't over—you could be dating your sister."

"We aren't dating at this point. We know we need to think about that, but I have a good feeling. It's just got to work out. Mom, I'm in love with her, and it doesn't feel sisterly." He let go of my hand and sat on the couch next to Sarah.

"I hope you're right, but I'm not sure Sam would be ready to be your dad. He's pretty mad that I didn't tell him about you."

"Mom, I need to know who my dad is, but not because I need someone to play catch with or hang out with—I need to know for me and Annie. Frankie or Sam will never take the place of my 'real' Dad. Paul raised me, and he was my 'real' dad no matter what the DNA says."

"You're right, Justin, you couldn't have asked for a better father than Paul." I explored his dark eyes. I wondered again if he'd inherited them from Frankie or if my brown eyes formed the dominant gene in a pairing with blue-eyed Sam? No matter where he got them, they looked to be in serious pain right now, contradicting his cheery smile. "But Paul is gone now. Sam is a good guy, and even if he never forgives me, I think he could be a good friend to you. You two have a lot in common."

"One more reason to believe Sam is my father. Frankie seems more like you with his English degree. You know he's written a screenplay and Annie says it's damn good." Justin laid his head back on the couch, pushed his dark mop of hair off his forehead, and closed his beautiful, brown eyes.

"Don't fall asleep there, kid. I need more information about this screenplay. I had no idea Frankie had that in him." There was so much I didn't know about Frankie. Had he grown up and become a responsible adult? I was a little jealous that he might have more talent than me. I had been writing for years—too afraid to risk the rejection of actually submitting my novel. "What's his screenplay about?"

"It has something to do with child abuse and domestic violence. I wonder why he chose such a dark subject."

"We write what we know," I said.

"What does that mean?" Justin looked concerned. "Did he abuse you, Mom?"

"Oh, no, he wouldn't think of hurting a woman, not after witnessing the abuse his mom took from his dad." I remembered the first time he told me about his younger years. "The only reason he ended up in Seattle is because his mom feared for his safety and sent him up here to live with his Aunt Betty."

Sarah had been sitting quietly reading the letters, but she decided to join the conversation. "Frankie had a shitty childhood and wouldn't think of physically abusing a woman, but I always thought he played a lot of mind games with you."

"And I let him. I don't think he ever meant to hurt me, but he did like to have his own way. I always gave him a free pass because of his childhood—well, almost always—he finally pissed me off on graduation night." My mind drifted back to that time. "And I never gave him a chance to explain."

"He'd have just made more excuses." Sarah smiled. "Honestly, I'm glad you broke up with him before you left, or you'd never have found Paul. He was a much better match for you."

"I can't dispute that." I smiled, too. "The best seventeen years of my life."

"And mine," Justin added as he got up to head to bed. "You and Dad gave me the best childhood a kid could ask for. I'm sorry the rest of you had such a tough one."

I stood up and hugged my boy—such a forgiving soul—after I put him through this ordeal, he continued to find kind words for me. "Goodnight, kid, you know I love you so much."

"I love you, too, Mom, no matter what happens."

Chapter Fifteen
Reminiscing

Tears fell from my eyes with the force of a summer rainstorm. There was no reason to hold back now that my son was off to bed. I did not have to be strong for Sarah or David. They knew the toll these past few days had taken on me, not that the previous twenty-five had been without challenges, but bringing all the missing pieces together at once was almost too much to bear.

"Hey, Sis, it's almost over and we just gave you good news." Sarah stood up and reached for my hand, pulling me from the recliner and moving me over to the couch where she cradled my head on her shoulder.

"I know. I'm happy about Dad, but I'm so worried about Justin." I curled up in a ball, not unlike one of Sarah's cats, leaning into her for comfort. "And I'm just sick about Sam. He means more to me than I realized."

Sarah stroked my dark mane of wavy hair, then took my face in both of her hands. "You're going to be okay, Jamie. You're doing the right thing even if Frankie and Sam are a little pissed that it took you so long."

"A little pissed? That's an understatement." Their reactions were different, but both were more than a little pissed. Frankie cried and lamented over what could have been. Sam just cut me off. I guess his desire for children and his ex-wife's betrayal were still too fresh. Why would he want another lying bitch in his life? I wondered if that was how he saw me now.

"I still believe everything will work out the way it is supposed to work out." No matter what happened, Sarah was always the optimist.

Uncurling my body, I rolled to a sitting position. "Thanks for your support. I don't know what I'd do without you." I hugged Sarah, holding on for a few extra seconds. The touch of her fingers on the back of my neck felt warm and gentle coaxing the tears that lived so close to the surface tonight from my swollen eyes. I pulled away and gathered the letters, placing each one into the old shoebox. "Time for me to take these letters and my bad attitude to bed. Goodnight you two." As I left the couch, Delilah took my place curling up beside Sarah as Sarah curled into David. A picture of the life I missed and a life I hoped to have again one day.

****

After washing off what was left of my makeup and brushing my teeth, I crossed the hall and slipped between the satin sheets. The three pillows encased in their yellow wraps needed fluffing if I was to form a proper backrest. I punched the first pillow with both hands as I imagined Frankie's chest at the other end of my fists; I wanted to pound on him for sharing our secret prematurely. Punching the second pillow with more force, I visualized Marcia's mean-spirited, gossipy mouth as my target. And finally, I lifted the last one, whacking it over and over and over, harder and faster, until there was no more strength in my wasted fist, then I took the pillow in my arms and clung to it with my last ounce of energy—that pillow was Sam.

The anger expended on the pillows built a plush wall to sink into as I finally laid back to read the first letter from Dad. My heart thumped with the same intensity as my fists beating the three fluffy pillows, but I was ready. With trembling fingers, I opened the first one, dated August 6, 1990, three days after my departure from Seattle.

Dear Jamie,

I can't stop thinking of your face as we watched you board the plane for Berkeley. I saw the fear in your eyes, but I think I saw a spark of hope and excitement as you set forth on your new adventure. I know you can do this, sweetie, and I will be with you all the way. We don't have a lot of extra money, so I hope the scholarship will provide what you need, but I promise to send you a letter every week to remind you that you have what it takes to turn this situation into something good. You've got spunk, Jamie, and that is what sets you apart from the rest. You were always studious like me, but you were never quiet, so use that voice to make new friends and be the best, most vibrant Jamie you can be.

Soon you will be bringing a new life into the world. I wish I could be there to see my first grandchild, but until your mother changes her view of the world, I will have to settle for your letters. Please write to me at work. The address is on the envelope.

I really want to know how you're doing, sweetie. I know I'm not physically there for you, but I want to be there, and I hope that is enough for now.

I Love you,

Dad

The next letter was dated a week later...

Hi Sweetie,

I haven't heard from you. I know you're probably busy settling in. I hope you're enjoying college life and making new friends. It must be hard to leave all of your old ones—you're really starting completely over. I didn't grasp the impact of this situation until now. How alone you must feel and how angry you must be at your Mom...and me.

I hope you will forgive me and let me be your link to sanity. Please write back, Jamie. I want to be there for you—I really do—but this is the best I can do for now.

Love you so much,

Dad

He did love me. If I'd seen these letters, it wouldn't have healed the wound completely, but it would have opened the door to saving my relationship with my father. I read the next few letters, feeling his pain with each word he wrote. As I read the letters, I still couldn't understand how he could let my mother have her way, and I had to admit that his weakness disappointed me. Why didn't he stand up to her? Why didn't *I* stand up to her? Looking back, it felt like we were all in a cult and Mom was the charismatic leader—and we all drank the Kool-Aid.

There were more letters from Dad, always hopeful that I would answer, but in the last one, four months later, he finally gave up hope.

Dear Jamie,

I hope you got the birthday card I sent from the office. They have the cutest little gift shop in the building, and when I saw that card, I thought of you. The little girl running through the field reminded me of your free spirit. And now you are eighteen—really free and independent.

Your mother found out I was writing to you. Surprisingly, she was not mad, but she pointed out that you're probably not interested in having a relationship with me. Everything I know about you tells me this could not be true, but it's been four months and you haven't written, so maybe she's right. She said you wanted to cut the ties and move on and we should do the same. God, I don't want to do that, but I guess I should respect your wishes.

I just want you to know I will never blame you for cutting the cord. You have every right to be mad at me for not taking a stand, but I fear it isn't anger you feel but disappointment and that's even harder to accept.

Sarah told me she's been in contact with you, so at least I know you're okay. Please don't let go of her. She is a good girl and loves you very much.

Maybe someday you will forgive me and let me back into your life. Until then, please just know that I love you with all my heart and will never let go of that love. You are my daughter and the blood that binds us is strong.

Be safe and raise your child with love. I'm sure you will do a better job than your mother and I did with you.

Love,

Dad

Would it have made a difference if those letters had arrived and I had stayed connected to Dad? I remember how lonely and lost I felt when the plane landed in Oakland. The bus was waiting to carry me and my limited belongings to my small apartment in Berkeley.

Being pregnant, I wasn't allowed in the dorm, but the scholarship provided enough for a cheap, one-bedroom unit that became home for me and my son for the next two years.

There wasn't anything Dad could have done, but it would have been nice to get those letters—to feel connected to my home. Maybe it made me stronger to forge ahead on my own, but in those early days in the starkly furnished apartment, my tears came easily and often. No family and the heightened hormone level brought on by my pregnancy made it hard to keep my mind on school. That's when I finally called Dad's Aunt Dorothy and took the bus to Oakland to meet her. We talked for hours about Dad and what a sweet kid he had been, but I wondered why I hadn't had any contact with her over the years. She told me she was the black sheep of her family—just like me—but, the main reason I'd never met her is that my Mom didn't like her and thought she'd be a bad influence on her children. Nothing could have been further from the truth. That day, Aunt Dot, as she preferred to be addressed, told me something that got me on the right track.

"Life is too short to carry around anger and bitterness. This is tough, but you need to let it go and move forward. Your mother sees the worst in every person and situation, maybe because she had a terrible childhood. She is damaged goods, but she hasn't broken you." She wrapped her fleshy arm around my shoulder and pulled me closer. "You can have happiness in this life, but you have to start today. Don't wait for some arbitrary day in the future to define your happiness—look for the good every day and if you don't see anything good, fake it. If you keep a positive outlook, one day you'll find you will no longer need to fake it; you will truly be happy." She hugged me and I felt her soft, round curves against my growing belly. Her curly, red hair came straight from a bottle of hair dye, an obvious attempt to defy her sixty years. When I studied her dark brown eyes, I was reminded of Dad, until I got to the blue eye shadow that made them her own. Honestly, she looked a little cheap with her low-cut blouse and tight stretch pants, but there was nothing tacky or cheap in the heart of the sweet woman I met that day.

I loved Aunt Dot's positive attitude, but I couldn't muster a smile. "That sounds good in theory, but have you looked at my life? I'm seventeen, pregnant, and alone. What have I got to smile about?"

"Plenty, Miss Jamie. You're alive and healthy and you need to stay that way for the little life growing inside you. Just, smile, damn it, and you'll be surprised at what comes your way."

Because of my mom's warning, I had been sure I would be shunned by all the self-respecting students and teachers, but that was not the case. As it turned out, Aunt Dot was right. Even though I was faking it at first, I smiled and talked to classmates and was indeed surprised to find that I could laugh again. That change in attitude opened the door to a new group of friends who helped me through my pregnancy and beyond.

And of course, Aunt Dot stayed on my radar. She was only a short bus ride away, and I used my bus pass often to go visit her in those first few years. She was eighty-five now, but I knew she'd be waiting for me when I returned, dying to find out the results of the paternity tests.

Remembering my time with Aunt Dot, and the friends I still called my guardian angels, set my heartbeat back to a peaceful level. I laid back on the marshmallow-soft pillows and closed my eyes. There had been some good in my day after all and now perhaps sleep would come.

No such luck, all I could think about was my mother, the woman who denied me peace even in death. I still resented her for not being there for me. She had nurtured me for seventeen years through illness, injury, and heartbreaks, but when I needed her the most, she was not there. So many times, I wanted to call Mom and beg her to let me and Justin come home, but my pride trumped my loneliness. Calling Sarah as often as my budget would allow, I more often settled for writing letters documenting my life and reporting every new achievement of my beautiful son. And whenever I felt especially lonely, I held Justin close to my heart, basking in the smell of baby lotion mixed with spit up, wondering if I had cheated him. What kind of life could I give him in my crappy, barren apartment, devoid of a father and an extended family? Every day I hated my mother more for the excommunication—I hated her and missed her at the same time—I needed my mommy...and my daddy.

And now after twenty-five years, I would have my daddy back. I couldn't wait until tomorrow...

Chapter Sixteen
No More Guilt

A bright, white ray of sunshine poked through the curtain and hit my eye like a lighthouse beacon. Had I even slept? The last time I looked at the clock on the night table, it was two o'clock a.m. and now I looked over and saw it was only seven o'clock a.m. It was Sunday, damn it, I wanted to go back to sleep. I deserved a few more hours of escape. Pulling the blanket over my head didn't help—the light rammed its way through. This was Seattle, for God's sake; where were all the damn clouds?

It was no use—too much light—so, I figured I might as well get up and enjoy the sunny Seattle day. No smell of bacon or coffee. I guess it was up to me to get things started. My job was easier than expected. The coffee maker was loaded and merely needed me to push the start button. I could do that. During the ten-minute wait for the coffee to brew, I paced and felt jittery—I needed my caffeine. The aroma was intoxicating, but my impatience for this particular cup of coffee was over the top. I'd waited twenty-five years to reconnect with old friends and family, yet I couldn't wait ten minutes for coffee? I pulled the coffee pot from its perch and shoved the ceramic cup with the yellow rose pattern under the stream of brewing coffee until it was half full, then quickly made the exchange without spilling a drop as I put the pot back. I leaned against the marble counter and took a sip of the hot liquid. Ah, the taste, the smell, the rush of caffeine. I closed my eyes and savored the moment of silence with my precious addiction. If that was my worst obsession, I would be okay.

But was that my worst obsession? It seemed my every thought and dream for the last five years was about Paul—the day we met, our wedding day, his relationship with Justin—all the memories had been wonderful...until that final day.

"Hey, Sis, what got you up so early?" Sarah had slipped into the room so silently, I hadn't detected her presence. Was it because my eyes were closed or because my thoughts were so loud inside my head?

My eyes popped open at the sound of her voice. "I couldn't sleep. Thinking too much, I guess."

"You looked deep in thought just now. Anything you want to tell your big sister?"

"I was thinking about Paul, about the day I lost him."

"I'm sorry, Jamie. Do you want to talk about it? You never told me what happened. I never wanted to push you, but maybe it would help to get it out." She put her arm around me and guided me to the barstool. "Why don't we sit? I'll pour myself some coffee and get us each a blueberry muffin."

The coffee was burning a hole in my stomach so when she put the muffin in front of me, I broke off a piece and devoured it. I was feeling a little nauseous, so the combination of the acid-absorbing muffin and my sister's compassion was just what I needed.

"I've never told anyone this, but I've always felt a

lot of guilt over his death. I think I could have prevented it."

"How so? It was a kitchen fire, and Paul was cooking. How could that be your fault?"

"The grease on the stove was definitely Paul's doing. He was so sweet, cooking me breakfast as I spent a few more lazy minutes in bed—quite a few actually—I drifted back to sleep while he cooked the bacon. I woke up to my man leaning over me promising me fried eggs cooked in the delicious bacon grease if I could drag my sorry ass out of bed." I smiled as I remembered the look on his face. "He said he was hungry, but I made the fatal mistake of asking him if he was hungry for eggs or for his hot wife. I laughed, thinking he would just drag me out of bed and down to the kitchen, but the school year was over, and we had nowhere we needed to be, so he chose me over the waiting bacon grease. And while we made love, the grease ignited and set the house on fire."

"It's not your fault, Jamie. You can't feel guilty about loving your husband. You didn't leave the grease on the stove."

"But I knew Paul. He really was the absent-minded professor at times. I should have asked if the burner was off, but all I wanted to do was run my hands through his prematurely gray hair and gaze into his steel blue eyes. I remember thinking how lucky I was to have him in my life, and as we reached the peak of our lovemaking, I felt a sense of peace."

"You need to keep remembering that. That fire took hold so fast in your old house, even if you had just talked for a few minutes, the result might have been the same…and you wouldn't have that special memory.

How nice for him to have his last act be one of love."

"That wasn't his last act of love, though. When we smelled the smoke, we ran to the hall and the stairway was engulfed with smoke and flames. We were trapped." My pulse was racing as I recounted the day. "He ran back to the bedroom and grabbed two blankets and my phone that sat on the nightstand. He called 911, wrapped me in one blanket, and wrapped the other around himself as he carried me down the staircase. His feet were on fire and as hard as he tried to move his blistered feet through the pain, he stumbled. I jumped to the right on a flame-free step, but he fell the other direction into a fiery beam. He hit his head and fell to the bottom of the stairway only a few feet from the front door, unconscious and on fire. I opened my arms using my blanket like a pair of angel wings and fell on him to smother the flames. I was successful, but when I looked at his face, I knew the blow to his head may have been more devastating than the fire. I kissed his lifeless face, hoping he would come back to me, then laid my head on his cheek. I wanted to be his angel, to save him from that fiery hell, but I couldn't move. As we laid together for the last time, I felt his heartbeat against my chest. He was alive. He was still alive! I heard the door break down and saw a bright orange fireball rush by my face, and that's the last I remember."

"You were out for quite a while." Sarah was holding my hand and when I saw her tears, I let mine go. "Telling you that Paul was gone was the hardest thing I've ever had to do."

Waking up with her and Justin by my side, I felt like a piece of meat that had just been seared on the barbecue. I was disoriented, but I quickly figured out where I was—I just didn't know how long I'd been there. Was Paul in the next room? Or had the heartbeat I felt been his last. Looking at Justin's face, I knew the answer, but I asked Sarah to confirm the truth.

"You were so gentle with your words, Sarah. Thank you for being there for me then…and now."

"You know I'll always be there for you, Sis. I'm glad you finally shared the details of that day with me because I think I can help you more than ever now." She stood up and took my face in her hands. "I know you loved Paul and you lost him in such a tragic way, but don't ever blame yourself for his death. The only thing you are guilty of is loving him too much and that's not a bad thing." She moved her hands to my shoulders and looked me squarely in my eyes. "But Jamie, he's not coming back, and you need to move on with your life. He would want you to find happiness."

"I know you're right. I'm alive, but I really haven't been living." I took in a deep breath, and as I exhaled, it felt like I'd let the air out of a balloon about to burst. There was now a little more room to breathe, to live, to love. "Justin has been telling me that for a couple of years now, but I just couldn't let the past go. I guess it's time."

"Did I hear my name?" Justin walked into the kitchen in wrinkled shorts and his Giants T-shirt, his hair reflecting a rough night's sleep and his beard reflecting the absence of a good razor. "I guess I need to get up earlier if I want to avoid having you two talk about me."

Sarah stood up and hugged her nephew. "It's all good, Justin. We were just talking about what a good

155

kid you were and how you took care of your Mom after the fire."

"It's a two-way street, Aunt Sarah. Mom helped me as much as I helped her." He came over to me and squeezed me in his Mom smothering hug. "I took a little time away from Stanford, but they were understanding, and it didn't affect my scholarship. And once Mom was on her feet, I went back full-time, but she knew I wasn't that far away."

"And he came home every weekend for a while. I'm one lucky Mom."

"It was kind of selfish on my part." He looked at me with those soulful eyes. "I needed you just as much—losing Dad was such a blow."

Sarah, little Miss Sunshine, put an optimistic spin on it. "But at least you have *your* Dad back, Jamie. And Justin, you get to meet your Grandpa today."

"I can't wait." Justin's voice reflected his enthusiasm, and I knew he meant every word.

I spent the next hour helping Sarah prepare breakfast and the four of us enjoyed a happier banter at the breakfast table. It was as if I'd finally buried the past and was ready to live again.

My body felt detached as I viewed Justin, Sarah, and David through a lens no longer clouded with the smoke that had followed me for five years; I could breathe again. That moment, sitting at the breakfast table with my family, I knew I would look back on this day as the day my life changed course. No more self-pity—I would celebrate Paul's life rather than mourn it, and I would celebrate *my* life.

My first act of self-love was a hot shower, cleansing yesterday's thoughts from my mind as I washed dirt from the knees that had mashed the gravel in the reunion parking lot last night. All traces of yesterday were swept down the drain, and when I emerged from the shower, I saw myself in the steamy mirror. I still had the scars, but somehow, they didn't look as bad today. When I looked at them, all I saw was love. I had fought to save my husband, and these were my battle scars. And although I didn't win that battle and Paul died despite my efforts, I would go on to fight another day.

But then the knock came on the bathroom door. The fight would not begin on another day—it was waiting just outside the door and down the hall.

Chapter Seventeen
Frankie's Plea

"Mom." Justin knocked a little louder. "Frankie's here. He says he needs to see you."

"Really?" Couldn't he wait until tomorrow when we would have the DNA results? "Tell him I'll be there in a minute. Get him a cup of coffee and keep him company for a few minutes."

I was still pretty pissed at him for last night's revelation—probably to our whole class. Why Marcia would want everyone to know her husband might be the father of my son was beyond me, but it seemed she wanted me to pay for winning his heart so many years ago and wanted Frankie to pay for breaking her heart so recently. At this point, I didn't care about Marcia—the competition was over—and right now, I didn't give a shit what Frankie thought of me, so I just dried my hair and put on a touch of mascara. I pulled on the blue capris and white T-shirt I'd brought into the bathroom, leaving my scar only half covered. If he was going to surprise me, he would have to take me the way I was. I brushed my teeth, dabbed a little gloss on my lips to give me a little color—maybe I cared what he thought just a little—and marched out to the man I would never understand. How was he going to talk his way out of this one?

Justin and Frankie seemed to be having a pleasant

exchange as I entered the room, but Justin was quick to jump up and head back toward his room. "Got some things to do before Grandpa gets here. See you later, Mom. Nice talking to you, Frankie." He rushed by me rather quickly as I continued toward my old flame.

Frankie's eyes opened a little wider as they found the red-wizened skin on my left arm. His brow furrowed momentarily as his smile faded, then in typical Frankie style, his expression reverted to his happy face—as if he had shaken the Etch A Sketch to remove the offensive picture and redrawn the perennial charming smile that defined him. It was a good save, but I saw the look, and I had to admit it hurt, but not as much as his betrayal the night before. He walked toward me as I entered the living room.

"Hey, kiddo, how are you doing this morning?" That damn cheery voice sent the message that all was well. Was this guy that clueless?

"Not so great, Frankie, no thanks to you and your big mouth."

"I probably shouldn't have said anything to Marcia, but I thought she should know." He reached for my hand, and I pulled it away with purpose.

"Why, Frankie? Why did Marcia need to know this before tomorrow? You already told Annie and you're divorcing Marcia, for God's sake. You don't owe her a thing. And her vindictive actions ruined the reunion for me." I moved to the recliner, so there would be no chance for him to touch me or try to persuade me to buy his explanation. He sat on the couch, turning sideways to face me as I spoke. "I should have been the one to tell Sam, not Marcia."

"He was going to find out soon enough. Marcia

saved you a difficult conversation."

"God, Frankie, you really don't get it. This isn't something you want to find out on the gossip chain. I should have told him."

"Why do you care so much? Are you in love with Sam?" he taunted. "What about us?" He gave me the look that used to melt me and this time I resisted.

"Do you really want us to get together? Aren't you mad as hell that I kept this secret from you?"

"Of course I'm mad, but I can't stay mad at you. You put up with my shit all through high school, and now it's my turn to accept some of yours."

"This is a pretty big piece of shit." I thought about Sam's reaction and wondered why Frankie had been so accepting. I guess I should have been happy for that, but it felt like he had lost his hot Italian passion. "Why are you so calm about all this?"

"What can I do? I was such a hothead in high school, I don't want you to see me like that. I want you to see that I've changed."

I looked at him. This was not the same guy I knew in high school, but I wasn't sure I liked the change. "Why do you need me to see that?"

"Because I need you back in my life. You always kept me out of trouble and led me down the right road. You were good for me…much better than Marcia." His smile faded as he said the words.

"You make me sound like a dose of medicine. I don't want to be your healthy choice for a nice bland life. I want passion, and I don't think you feel that for me."

He stood up, pulled me from the chair, and placed my hands on his shoulders. This time I did not resist.

He held my face in his warm grip for only a second before he found my lips with his warm searching mouth, and as he let go of my face and wrapped his arms around my waist, I felt a hint of the passion of our youth. Only a hint. It was a nice kiss, even a little arousing, but it wasn't Sam's kiss. That was the kiss I wanted—I knew that now. I pulled away, and I rested my head on Frankie's shoulder. After a few minutes, I reached behind me and took his hands in mine.

"Frankie, when I left you twenty-five years ago, I thought of you every day wondering if I'd made the right decision. I missed you so much, and I really believed I loved you despite your flirtations with Marcia." Studying his face, the new grown-up face, I saw a tamed down version of my high school Frankie. "And now I can say without a doubt, that I do love you, but I don't want to start over with you, and I don't think you want that either—you just think you do." His head dropped down, avoiding my eyes. "Do you still love Marcia?"

"Of course not!" He protested a little too loudly.

"Really? I saw you with her, and to be honest, I think she has always been your passion. You and I were great friends, and we were good for each other, but there is a difference between loving someone and being *in love*."

He dropped my hands and turned away, trying to hide the pain I saw etched in his face the moment before he turned. Without looking at me, he spoke quietly. "I did love her at one time. I loved her very much. But she's not an easy person to love, you know."

"You don't have to convince me of that. She was my best friend all through grade school, and I loved her

161

as much as a kid could love a friend from age five through age eleven—that was when she moved on." I walked around to face Frankie. "I know her better than you think I do. She has always wanted acceptance, and for some reason, she wanted it from the more popular kids, including you. It hurt that she left me behind, but knowing her family, I think I understand her need for attention. I just wish she hadn't carried that need into last night. I'm sure everyone is talking about it."

"She only told Sam. No one else has a clue."

"You're kidding? Why would she do that to Sam?"

"She didn't even think of Sam's feelings; she was just trying to get to you. She was jealous, kiddo. She saw us dancing, and she wanted to find a way to get you out of the way and it worked. She's always been jealous of my feelings for you."

"It sounds like she still loves you. And from that tear in your eye, I think you love her, too."

"I don't want to love her. She's been a pain in my ass from the day I met her. I want someone nice like you." He grabbed my arm—the sensitive, burned arm—and I let out a yelp.

He let go quickly. "Sorry, Jamie. Are you all right? Maybe you should cover that up."

I rubbed the sore flesh. "Why? So you don't have to look at it? This is me, Frankie. This is what you get if you want me."

"Can't you get it fixed like you did your face?" He touched my smooth cheek. "You look so beautiful now."

"Now? I take it you like the new nose better than the old one." I had to admit, I liked the change, but did he have to focus on my looks?

He stumbled over the words. "I…I loved your old nose, but, I mean, you were able to fix your scars and that's a good thing, isn't it?"

"Yeah, it's a good thing, but I don't plan to fix my arm and leg. Do you have any idea how painful all those surgeries were? I'm done fixing the outside. I'm going to start working on the inside."

"Good idea, kiddo. You know I'd love you no matter what you looked like. You do know that, don't you?"

"Sure, Frankie. I know that." But I really wasn't sure. After all, he had always been distracted by beautiful Marcia, even when we were a couple all those years ago. Was Frankie a little more superficial than he wanted to admit? I certainly thought so, and this little exchange of words solidified that feeling.

The silence between us was unusual, but I didn't know what more to say after his comments. Was I being overly sensitive? Maybe. I looked at the ground rather than look back into his eyes. I didn't want him to try to convince me that I was wrong about this. He was too good at giving me the hard sell, and in my heart, I knew he would never really believe I was beautiful. I might have been good for him and he might have been very happy with me, but I would never be a "ten" in his eyes, and I wanted to be with someone who saw me as beautiful inside and out—someone who saw me as their "ten."

"Hey, Mom, we need to go to the store to get some stuff for the barbecue today." Saved by my son. "Sorry you guys, but we need to get going." Had he been in the kitchen all along, listening to our conversation?

"Oh, no problem. I was just leaving. Nice to see

you, Justin." Frankie reached out to shake Justin's hand—a little formal for the guy I remembered—but my well-mannered son responded and gripped his hand firmly. Then Frankie pulled me in awkwardly and gave me a hug which I returned, more from obligation than desire. "See you tomorrow, kiddo."

"Yeah, tomorrow…" God, I wasn't ready for the results of the DNA test, but it was time to get to the end of the pain. "See you tomorrow." I walked him to the door and held it open as I watched him walk away. This handsome, sexy man could be mine if I wanted him, but did I want him? Would he ever love me the way I wanted and needed to be loved?

****

"I'll drive. You've been hoarding the car all week, Mom." Justin waited for me to hand him the keys which I did after hitting the button to unlock the doors. I didn't know much about cars, but this little green blob looked like a frog waiting to suck us into the tiny cockpit. Once we were both stuffed into our polyester upholstered bucket seats, I opened the glove box and looked at the manual—a Ford Fiesta—we didn't need a big car, but this was more than compact. Didn't Fiesta mean a big elaborate party or festival? I wondered how they came up with such a big name for this gutless little vehicle.

"Hey, Mom, you're awfully quiet." He adjusted the mirror and started the engine, continuing the conversation as he backed out of the driveway. "What's going on with you and Frankie? Are you getting back together after all these years?"

"I don't know. I think he'd like that, but I'm just not sure." I looked at Justin. "How would you feel if he was your father?"

"If it weren't for Annie, I'd be okay with it. I like Frankie, but Mom, I don't think he's right for you."

"Why do you say that?"

"Because I overheard most of your conversation and I don't think he's in love with you. I think he thinks he is, but honestly, he's a little self-centered and is just looking out for himself. He wants a nice stable relationship, and it doesn't sound like he had that with Marcia."

"You're probably right. How did you get to be so smart at the tender age of twenty-four?" I reached into my purse to check my phone. No new texts. "Frankie's a good guy, though. I could do worse."

"But you could also do better, and I'm not saying that Frankie isn't a great guy, but I mean you should hold out for someone you really love. I don't think you're in love with him."

"How do you know so much about love, young man?"

"I saw you with Dad for seventeen years—that was love. And sadly, it's also because of Annie. I've never felt this connected to anyone in my life and I hope to God it not because we're related." He glanced over to me as we stopped at a red light. "Please tell me there's something in me that reminds you of Sam."

"There is." I saw it now. "Sam is the kindest man I have ever known. Like you, he is honest, compassionate, loving, and the best friend a girl could ever have. Plus, he makes me laugh. You are very much like Sam."

"Mom? Look at me." He searched my eyes. "You're in love with Sam, aren't you?"

165

"I didn't think so. I always thought he was just a friend, but I miss him so much now that he's out of my life." I looked at my phone again, hoping for a text from Sam. Could he just walk away?

"Do you really think he'll hold this against you? Doesn't he know how hard this has been for you?"

"I think he'd be happy to be your father, but he never had children and if you are his son, he'll probably be even madder. I mean, how would you feel if you missed out on your child's first twenty-four years?" It had been selfish of me to keep this from him and the guilt felt like a giant boulder weighing on my chest. "His ex-wife lied to him about her ability to have children, and I never told him the truth about you, so he's not in a good place right now."

"I'm sure he'll come around. I hope so for your sake, Mom. It seems like you really have it bad for the guy."

"I don't know. When Sam makes up his mind about something, it's pretty hard to get him to change it." I smiled just thinking about all the years he told me Frankie was not right for me—he would not budge on his opinion—and it looked like he was right.

I just hoped that Sam would not hold so tight to his opinion of my perceived dishonesty. Maybe some of his kindness and compassion would override his stubborn logic.

"You're pretty awesome, Mom. If he doesn't see that, he's not worth your time."

"That's where you're wrong, kid. He's worth so much more than I ever realized." I didn't want Justin to see me cry, so I looked out my window. Staring at the rundown shops on Highway 99, the route to Costco, reminded me just how many years had passed. The little music store where I had taken my first piano lesson was now a Teriyaki takeout joint. Where had the years gone?

Justin hated to see me cry, so he did what he always did; he tried to cheer me up. Turning up the volume on the radio didn't bring the results he hoped for—the oldies station that was still on the tuner was playing "You've Lost That Loving Feeling" by The Righteous Brothers—the lyrics felt like a knife to my already broken heart. As my son quickly flipped to a current pop/rock station, the song choice wasn't much better—"Somebody that I Used to Know" by Gotye. The title made me think of both Frankie and Sam, but the tune was so catchy, and the words so snarky, that I started to laugh, and Justin and I sang our way to Costco.

There would be time to deal with our love lives later. So much depended on the outcome of events tomorrow. Maybe we would both live happily ever after or maybe we would both need to start over. But for now, we would sing our way down the highway and then stroll through Costco gathering a rack of their fabulous ribs, chips, supplies for Sarah's famous potato salad, a ripe watermelon, and a case of gourmet beer Justin assured me everyone would love.

Today, we would celebrate. On this day, Justin would meet his grandpa, my dad.

And as I looked at my boy walking toward me with the watermelon in hand, I saw it. Looking at his thick crop of dark hair and his long Romanesque nose, I realized who he looked like, and it wasn't Frankie or Sam, it was his grandpa, Jack Madison. It would be nice to see the two of them together today.

Chapter Eighteen
Dad's Home

The smoky scent of coals smoldering on the old-fashioned barbecue sent my mind back thirty years. Reclining on the soft cushion of silky sunflowers, pleasant memories from childhood filled my head...

Every weeknight promptly at five fifty p.m., Dad walked through the front door of our small, yellow rambler, and every night, I announced to Mom and Sarah, "Dad's home!" The bus always dropped him at the top of the hill on schedule and his jaunty step from the bus stop to the door brought him home to us at the same predictable hour. I thought of Dad as I looked out Sarah's picture window, remembering how I'd watch him walk up the driveway, a lock of his dark hair falling onto his forehead. He'd slick it back in the morning for work, but at the end of the day, it would always fall loose, much like his grandson, Justin's unruly shock of hair. My mind drifted back to those days, remembering that even though his entrance was expected, there was not a night that I found his arrival anything short of wonderful and worthy of my declaration. The ritual began at about age five and continued through high school, and as annoying as Mom and Sarah found the repetitive proclamation, I think they missed my words the last two weeks I was at home. But I didn't want to think about those last two weeks, I wanted to remember the three thousand plus days I announced, "Dad's home!" and the evenings we shared.

Mom always had dinner on the table when he arrived. She gave Dad no more than ten minutes to change from his business suit into his white T-shirt and jeans, because apparently, we needed to be in our seats before the clock struck six p.m. Why the schedule was so tight I never knew, but we didn't question it; we just sat our butts in the red vinyl chairs at the small faux wood kitchen table and waited for Mom's simple but delicious home cooking. Even though money was tight, we always ate well because Mom knew how to make the cheapest cut of meat into a tender pot roast and could complement any meal with macaroni and cheese that put Kraft to shame. The aroma of the roasting meat still filled my head years after leaving home. Matching Mom's culinary skills was never something I aspired to, but I often missed our cozy little kitchen.

To be honest, food wasn't the driving force behind my love of the dinner hour. It was Dad's dinnertime recitals that brought joy to me each night. In deference to Mom, he would start out by asking, "How was your day, Nancy?" after which she would sometimes recount a good day playing bridge with her best friends Mary, Vi, and Carol, but more often she would find a reason to complain about one of the other neighbors or the butcher or the grocer or whoever crossed her path in the wrong direction. He let her go on for a good five minutes and when she stopped to take a breath, he turned to Sarah to ask, "How many more young boys' hearts did you break today, Miss Sarah?" She would always blush, but then proceed to let us know all about her newest beau. Then it was my turn, "What did you learn in school today my little Jamie?" I loved my five minutes of attention and always made sure I had something new to tell him. And he was always quick to tell me he was proud of me and knew I would grow up to be either a rocket scientist or a famous author, a testament to the fact that I used both sides of my brain.

And Dad used both sides of his brain, the left side for work at a financial institution each day and the right side to recite poetry or some interesting prose each night at the dinner table. Although he never brought a book to our meal, he could recite hundreds of poems from memory. That was the birth of my love for literature. Learning that I was the "master of my fate" and "the captain of my soul" through the words in the poem *Invictus* still stuck in my brain today, maybe especially today. *Invictus* was one of Dad's favorites, and I needed to thank him for giving me strength with that emotional piece as well as so many others. How could I have doubted the man who infused the love of words into my heart?

And now, as I lay spent on Sarah's yellow-flowered recliner, my thoughts were interrupted by the familiar knock—Rat tata tat tat...tat tat. Although the sound was muted, I jumped as if a firecracker had exploded on the front porch. Dad was here!

"Dad's home!" I yelled with the enthusiasm of my ten-year-old self. In that moment, all the lost years evaporated as I opened the door and sought my father's aging brown eyes. One look told me all I needed to know. He loved me.

As I reached for him, his arms flew around me like the wings of a proud eagle, his baby bird back in the fold. Holding me tight, he trembled, then released a sigh that felt like the weight of the world had been lifted from his shoulders. I buried my face in his chest, clinging to the man who had been my security blanket for the first seventeen years of my life. Now I knew he had wanted to be there for the last twenty-five; the letters showed me he had at least tried to be there. We lost those years, but we would not lose another minute.

"I'm sorry, Dad. I'm sorry I doubted you."

He loosened his grip and brought his hands to my face, cupping my cheeks with his warm fingers. His eyes sought mine. "You have nothing to apologize for, sweetie. I'm the one who should be sorry—and I am— I'm so sorry I wasn't there for you when you needed me most."

"It's okay." My voice was soft and hesitant as I looked down.

"No, it's not. I let you down." He lifted my chin to bring my eyes back to him, and I saw his pain. "I think I finally get it, sweetie—you were right. The longer I'm alone, the more peace I feel, but God help me, I still miss your mother."

"I guess we can't help who we love, even if they're bad for us." I thought of Frankie and realized I was a lot like my dad. I stayed in a dysfunctional relationship all through high school, and if my mother hadn't thrown me out, I could easily have suffered the same contrary life my parents endured.

"Mom?" I hadn't heard Justin walk up behind me. Letting go of Dad, finally, I turned to face my son.

"Justin, I'd like you to meet your grandpa, Jack Madison." Their eyes were already locked on each other. Justin held his hand out for a formal handshake and my dad made me proud, bypassing his hand and gripping him in a heartfelt hug. My son did not resist. I stepped back and observed the connection between the two men who meant so much to me.

Justin spoke first. "So, Grandpa, Mom says you're a genius, a member of Mensa. So, if you're so smart, why did you stay with Grandma?"

That was a bit rude, and I started to make a move to call him out, but Dad waved me off and answered. "Lots of book smarts, son, but no common sense when it came to women, especially your grandma."

We all laughed, then the three of us walked arm in arm in arm to the backyard where the ribs were about to meet the barbecue grill. Sarah greeted us as we squeezed through the sliding glass door opening, still clinging to one another. Adding herself to the human chain, we pulled together into a group hug. David just smiled at us from his post in front of the barbecue, and as we wound ourselves around the glass patio table, we finally detached our interwoven arms. But I couldn't completely detach; I gently put Dad's hand between both of mine and held it as if I was cradling an injured kitten. We had all been injured in this ordeal, but it was time to heal.

Justin remained standing as did Sarah. "Let me get you a beer, Grandpa."

"Sounds good. And how about one for your mom and aunt?" Always looking out for his girls—except for that twenty-five-year break with me—but still…

Sarah gave me a look. "I know you're not a big beer drinker, Jamie. I'll grab you an iced tea."

"Since when don't you like beer, Mom?"

"Since I came home to all this stress, kiddo. I think

a beer would knock me out. Iced tea sounds great, Sarah." She knew me so well, and she was right that I just couldn't handle alcohol right now.

Dad and I were discussing Sarah's passion for yellow as displayed in the lemon-colored patio cushions, placemats, and umbrella when Justin and Sarah returned with our drinks, which just happened to be in clear plastic tumblers with yellow and orange polka dots. I had to admit, the yellow accents had helped my mood these past few days, but the man in the blue polo shirt and plaid shorts was the brightest accent in my life today. Dad always called me his little ray of sunshine, and today he was mine. But I had a few questions.

I finally let go of his hand so he could partake of the microbrew Justin insisted on buying, and I took a long drink of the cool, lemony, sweet, iced tea. It was time to talk. "I read your letters last night, Dad. They were beautiful." He smiled as I continued. "But I don't understand why Mom held those back and let the ones with the money get through. Did you send those from work?"

"What money?"

"The hundred-dollar bill you sent every month. I never could understand why you folded it in a plain sheet of paper—no note—and risked sending cash in the mail." His expression told me he didn't remember these details. Was he losing his memory? God, I just found him again—what a cruel twist of fate if I lost him to Alzheimer's. What a waste of his perfect, intelligent brain. "Dad? Don't you remember those neatly typed envelopes? Did you send them from your office?"

"I didn't send them, Jamie." His voice was quiet as

his eyes turned downward.

"What do you mean? Of course, it was you, I mean, who else could have sent them? You and Mom and Sarah were the only ones who knew where I was." I lifted Dad's chin and searched his eyes. They looked bright for a sixty-seven-year-old man, but maybe that wasn't the first sign. "Are you okay, Dad?"

"Of course, I'm okay. I did *not* send that money! I couldn't take the chance of your mom finding out. We never seemed to have much leftover at that point in our lives, anyway—even when Nancy went back to work. I don't know what she spent the extra money on…"

Sarah's eyes met mine, then moved to Dad. As I looked at Dad then back to Sarah, the three of us reached the same conclusion. I swear I saw a light bulb glowing above our heads as we voiced our shared revelation. "It was Mom!"

"So Grandma had a heart after all," Justin said with a bit of an edge to his voice. "Either that or she felt guilty."

"Oh my God! The woman who wouldn't talk to me for twenty-five years and would never admit she was wrong, apparently didn't want us to go hungry. I don't know what to think." I should have been happy to know my mother wanted to help me, but all I felt was a hot swirling sensation in my stomach that ascended through my chest to my now bright hot cheeks. "Damn her. Damn her to hell!" I screamed. "All those wasted years. Why didn't she tell me she was sending money?"

"Pride. Your mother had too much pride to make the first move. She was waiting for you to apologize."

"Why would I do that, Dad? Good God, she told me to get the hell out and never come back. What was I supposed to think? I was just a kid of seventeen and I wasn't about to cross Mom." I picked up my glass of iced tea and held the glass to my flushed face. Taking a long drink of the cool liquid, I closed my eyes. "God, I would have given anything to come home that first year."

Dad put his arm around my shoulder. "I'm sorry, sweetie. That wouldn't have happened. You know your mother could never admit she was wrong."

Looking up into his dark brown eyes, damp with tears held in check, I asked the hardest question. "Even when I was lying in the hospital, burned and widowed; she couldn't even come to me then?"

"I know you won't believe this, but I heard her crying at night, whispering your name. She didn't know I heard her. By day, she told me God was punishing you."

"Did you believe that?"

"Of course not. I was just too afraid to come to your side. I'm not proud of myself, but I called Sarah every day to check on you." A tear rolled down his cheek. "I really wasn't sure if seeing me after twenty years would have been a good thing. I didn't want to cause you any more stress during your healing."

Sarah chimed in. "I told her you called, Dad. It was the first thing I said that made her smile."

"I wish I could change the past. I didn't deserve your smile back then, but I'll do everything I can to make it up to you and Justin."

Justin put his arm around Dad's bony shoulder. "I'm just glad I finally get a chance to spend some time with my Grandpa." He looked Dad in the eye. "Grandma must have loved us a little to send the money, but I can tell you love us a lot, and I think I'm beginning to understand why you found it hard to cross her."

"You don't know the half of it," Sarah added. "There was no pleasing that woman. I don't think there was anything you or your mom could have done to heal the wound. She probably felt better sending you money, but I don't think she could have accepted you back into the family. It's pretty sad, really."

"Very sad." I hung my head thinking about all the lost years. "I just wish you could have met Paul, Dad." Thoughts of what might have been sent me sinking into the past, then I looked up and saw myself in Dad's face—the deep brown eyes, the high cheekbones, the rosy lips under a nose slightly too large for either face—and decided the time for sorrow was over. He was right, we couldn't change the past. I touched his cheek. "No more tears, Dad. It's time to move forward, and I'm going to start by moving my ass in the direction of the barbecue." I grabbed his hand. "C'mon. Let's go."

"I'm with you, Mom. Time to move those ribs from the grill to my mouth. I'm hungry."

After loading our plates with David's fabulous ribs and Sarah's signature potato salad and baked beans, we filled our stomachs with the comfort food. The conversations moved from the tragedy of past events to the joy of today's reunion. We laughed, we shared our stories, but most of all, we loved. We were a family again and a very happy one at that.

Chapter Nineteen
Who's Your Daddy?

Love comes in strange packages. True, I didn't have a romantic partner—Paul was gone, and neither Frankie nor Sam were going to fill that void—but I had two men in my life who gave me all the love I needed for now. Justin and Dad were the men in my life, and as I observed them earlier in the evening, I realized I was the conduit that passed Dad's honesty, integrity, and compassion to my son. Did Justin inherit anything from his biological father? From my vantage point, it seemed his humor and intellect came directly from Grandpa Jack. They were so much alike.

After a wonderful, but emotionally draining day, I hadn't been able to sleep, so I found my way outside to the chaise lounge on the patio. My red silk robe laid loosely across my damaged thigh as I counted stars, wishing upon the first that caught my eye. As a child, I'd stared into the same sky and felt so insignificant, but I didn't understand this little speck of human life that was me could hold the entire universe in her heart. Tonight with Dad, my heart opened like a blooming flower, inviting love in as I let go of the resentment and anger I'd been carrying for years. After twenty-five years of silence, the soothing sound of Dad's voice was like music to my waiting ears. A sweet song at first, growing as the day passed to a robust symphony filling that silence with love and joy. And giving my son the gift of his grandfather—even though it was a few years late—opened my heart even further.

The only person who kept me from a pure heart was Mom. Forgiving her was something I thought I could never do, but even *she* appeared to have a small conscience, and a minimally functional heart, as she sent the money to feed us all those years ago. Perhaps she did the best she could with her narrow and fearful view of life. It affected all of us—this family had been damaged by her actions—but each one of us could have called her bluff. We all played the game and let her control our lives, thinking that was what she wanted—to be the Queen Bee. But when I looked at her small act of kindness toward Justin and me, I wondered who she really was and if she wanted that at all. Maybe we could have changed things if we all said, "No more!" But we didn't, and she died an angry and unhappy woman.

I felt a chill in the night air, or was it coming from inside my heart as I admitted to myself that I could have done something. I was as stubborn as Mom, and as hard as it was to admit, it was clear that *I* was the selfish one. I blamed her for the estrangement and wore my victim mentality like a badge of honor, but the truth was, I could have come back and *should* have come back. But I didn't want to share my son with another man. Paul and I were happy, and Justin was Paul's son even if he hadn't planted the actual seed. This was my family, and I didn't want to disrupt it with a biological father who would take Justin away every month. Yes, I was the selfish one, and I made a choice to keep my secret from Frankie and Sam. In a few hours, I would pay the price for that long-kept secret.

****

Sarah had slipped silently out the door at seven a.m., heading for her lab where the DNA sample was tucked away in a secret alcove awaiting her analysis. Sweet of her to try not to wake us, but I'd only been back in bed for a few hours and it didn't feel like I'd slept more than five minutes at a time. Knowing our lives were going to change the moment Justin's paternity was determined, how could we sleep?

****

Justin and I looked at the clock on the wall as it chimed its hourly reminder that the morning was passing, and it was now ten a.m. Had Sarah's boss caught her running this test without the proper consent forms? Had someone found her secret spot and turned her in? No doubt the results were clear. This process only took twenty-four hours. Unfortunately, she started it Friday after her boss left for the day, and she couldn't risk sneaking in on Saturday or Sunday, so we'd endured two extra days of torture. Now we sat wordlessly watching the cell phone on the coffee table—willing it to ring, while secretly hoping it wouldn't.

The vibration followed by my annoyingly cheery ringtone came only a few minutes later, displaying Sarah's name on the previously blank screen. Justin and I looked at one another, but he was the brave one, and taking a deep breath, he tapped the screen putting Sarah on speakerphone.

"Okay, Aunt Sarah, I'm ready." His jaw barely moved as he clenched his teeth, waiting for the word.

"I'm not but go ahead." I grabbed Justin's hand and held tight.

Sarah cleared her throat then began. "The test results are clear." She hesitated, then spoke quietly. "Frankie is definitely…Justin's father. I'm so sorry."

"Nooooooo…" Justin's wail sounded more like the howl of a wounded animal than my sweet child. His moan filled the room as he pulled his hand from mine and rushed toward the window. His eyes turned toward the blue Seattle sky, he lifted his arms to the glass, his damp palms leaving their mark on the surface. "Why, God? Why would you do this to me? You took the only man I ever called Dad, let him burn in that awful fire, and now you replace him with the father of the girl I love. What kind of cruel joke is this?" His head fell against the window as I watched his body shake with sobs.

"I'm so sorry, Justin. I'm so, so sorry." There were no words to comfort him and none that would help this make sense to me. But as his mom, I had to try. I ran to the window and wrapped my arms around my son as I had done so many times in his youth. This was bigger than a skinned knee or even the broken nose he'd suffered in Little League—those had healed—this would change the course of his life. Annie was "the one." I had seen that in his eyes on the plane a few days ago. She was "the one," and I had ruined it, yet he clung to me as if I was his savior, holding me so tight I could barely breathe. "I'm so lucky to have you, Justin. I'm sorry Frankie is your father, but if he wasn't, you wouldn't be you—I need to thank him for that. His genes made you who you are as much as mine."

"You're right." He caught his breath as he continued to hug me. "But fuck science and all my perfect genes! If it weren't for Frankie, I wouldn't be

me, right? But I'm not sure I want to be me right now."
He loosened his grip and pulled away locking his
swollen eyes on mine. With one look, his pain pierced
my already breaking heart. I hadn't realized the depth
of his feelings until that moment. "I love Annie—my
goddamn sister—how sick is that? And now, I have to
tell her goodbye. This is just one big clusterfuck!"

He called that one. I could think of no better words
to describe our situation. And it wouldn't be getting any
easier as we prepared ourselves to deliver the news to
Frankie and Annie.

"Let's get going, kiddo." I chose that nickname for
my son the day he was born—an odd choice since I had
been mad at Frankie when I left Seattle. The truth was,
I always loved hearing that tag—it seemed endearing
without being sappy. So, I passed it on to Justin, and
over the years, he thanked me many times over for not
calling him honey or sweetie in front of his friends—
kiddo was just fine with him.

"You can drive." He tossed me the keys and we
headed for the green machine.

Justin stared out the window as I maneuvered the
Ford Fiesta through the streets of Shoreline toward
Frankie's childhood home. I was glad he was staying
there, a place I found familiar and peaceful as I
remembered the hours I spent with him and his Aunt
Betty. Now Betty and Ollie were off visiting their
native Italy while Frankie watched their golden
retriever, Sandy.

The ride was only fifteen minutes—not enough
time to erase the physical effects of the news. Justin
made no attempt to hide his eyes, removing
sunglasses as he bravely stepped from the car. He

headed for the front door.

"This way," I said, leading him around the back. I knew Frankie well enough to know he'd be in the backyard, where the sun found a way to sift through the mighty evergreens that lined the property. I glanced at the beloved rope swing as I turned the corner and was not surprised to see Frankie and Annie on the patio ahead waiting for us. Annie was taking a bite of a muffin as we came into view—her eyes moved upward taking us in—one look telling her all she needed to know. She sat motionless except for the slow, deliberate chewing action needed to dissolve the too-large bite of muffin.

Frankie ran to me, anticipating the news, placing his hand gently on my back as he guided me to the table where Annie was finally swallowing hard. Justin followed closely, never taking his eyes from his sister. I guess it was up to me to say what everyone already knew.

"Frankie, you *are* Justin's father. There is no doubt, according to the test—no doubt at all." I looked at Annie, the only one still sitting. The color drained from her face, her blue eyes filling with tears.

Annie was the quiet one of the bunch, but she spoke first. "Dad, I don't know what to say. I could say I wish you hadn't slept with Justin's mom, but then Justin wouldn't be here. It's kind of sick that I fell in love with my brother."

"You love me?" Justin obviously hadn't heard the words from her yet.

"I do, but I guess I'll have to rechannel that love in a…more sisterly way." She took Justin's hand. "Let's go talk, Justin. We're family now, right?"

183

"I'm sorry things turned out this way for you and Annie." Frankie reached toward Justin as he said the words. "But I'm glad to have you in our family."

"I hope you don't mind if I don't call you Dad—I know you're a nice guy and all—but, I'm not gonna lie, I wish you weren't my father." He didn't respond to Frankie's gesture.

"I understand." He dropped his hand. "You two go talk. I'll talk to your mom."

I knew Justin's remarks were rude, but I didn't blame him, and I hoped Frankie really did understand. It must have been hard for him on two counts. His daughter was disappointed, and his newfound son wanted nothing to do with him.

"I'm sorry, Frankie. There is no way to make this news good for anyone."

"It's funny," he said as he took my hands in his, "I always wanted a son and now that I have him, I would do anything to remove my DNA from him. I was really hoping that asshole, Sam, would be his father."

"Me, too, although I don't agree with you that he's an asshole. We all had a part in that night, and no one was any more to blame than the other."

"I just wish you'd never gotten pregnant. Maybe we would have had a future."

"But then I wouldn't have had Justin. And you must admit, we did an awesome job of combining our DNA to make that child. He's the best thing that ever happened to me."

"If you'd never gotten pregnant, you would never have known that."

"But I did, and I do. If I'd never had Justin, I think I would have known something was missing. How can you even think about a life without him?"

"I guess I'm being selfish."

I pulled my hands away. "Yes, you are. There was never any guarantee you and I would have gotten over that last breakup. And you would never have had Annie if you hadn't gotten together with Marcia."

"That's true. I just keep thinking all of our lives would have been better if the punch hadn't been spiked on graduation night."

"Different, maybe, but not better. I've had a pretty nice life and until recently it sounds like you've had a decent life, too."

"It's been okay, but I miss you, kiddo."

I took a deep breath. The scent of the evergreens drifting up from the gully brought back memories. "You know what I miss? I miss the rope swing and the carefree days we spent in this backyard. I miss all the neighborhood kids, even Marcia a little." I studied his sexy, dark eyes wondering why I didn't want more from him. "I miss you, too, but my life is so different now. We would never fit."

He closed his eyes. "You're probably right." When his eyes opened, he turned his gaze to the mighty evergreens, the sun filtering its rays through their branches. "Just tell me this, kiddo, what's Sam got that I don't have?"

I flinched at the question. "Where did that come from?"

"I'm not stupid. I can see it in your eyes when you talk about him." He grabbed my arm as he turned back toward me. "So, tell me. Why do you want him and not me?"

"I could ask you the same question about Marcia.

Maybe you don't see it, but you are not done with that woman."

"The hell I'm not! I can't take any more of our bickering."

"Really?" I broke away from his hold. "If I look back on our relationship, you seemed to thrive on that edge. I think you like that."

"You're wrong about that."

"I've heard that before. Maybe you've changed, but whenever we fought, I always walked away thinking I was wrong. I don't want to doubt myself like that anymore."

"I never meant to hurt you, kiddo."

"I know, but we're like oil and water—we don't mix. So, it's not what Sam has, it's what he doesn't have—the need fight."

"Well, isn't he just the perfect guy." Frankie's tone was more than sarcastic.

"Not really. He's got his flaws—he's not as forgiving as you are. The truth is, I'll probably never see him again now that you won the paternity test."

"I know this isn't funny, but I never thought I would do better on a test than Sam."

It was funny. I laughed, relieving some of the tension. "You won the prize. Justin is a great kid."

"Now I have two great kids, but I'm still missing that special woman."

"And I don't have that special man, but maybe we should just take some time for ourselves."

Frankie took my hand and led me to the porch swing. The dark, forest green cushion was plump with stuffing, and I wasted no time nestling my butt into the soft fabric. Frankie followed leaving no space between us. "I'll take time for myself tomorrow. Right now, I just want to hold you in my arms."

I laid my head on his chest as he wrapped his arms around me. His steady heartbeat had a calming effect as I closed my eyes and sank into him. Would this be the last time I felt his warm breath on the back of my neck? Would I miss him when I left on Saturday? Yes, I would miss the boy who changed my life so many years ago. Crossing my arms, I laced my fingers through his for one last time, silently thanking him for the gift he gave me twenty-five years ago.

Chapter Twenty
Sisterly Love

Frankie was the father of my son. Damn it! This was not the way it was supposed to turn out. I couldn't lie to myself, I enjoyed the feeling of his arms around me, but I couldn't quite wrap my arms around the concept that he would be in Justin's life from now on—and mine, too, for that matter. We were family.

This wasn't the family I pictured. My nest in his embrace was only a temporary resting place—now this baby bird needed to fly. Suddenly I couldn't wait to get out of there. I unraveled my fingers from his and jumped up like someone had stuck a firecracker in my pants.

"What's with you, Jamie?" He grabbed my hand trying to pull me back to him.

"I need to go." I pulled away. "I can't lay here pretending everything is fine when our kids are in agony."

"They'll get over it. They haven't been seeing each other that long."

"I don't think time has anything to do with love." I thought about how I'd fallen for Paul the minute I met him. We had married within six months and it had been right. "Some couples grow into love and others just know the minute they meet." I knew about the slow evolution of love, too. It had taken me twenty-five years to fall in love with Sam.

"I need to get out of here and tell Sam the news." I walked over to the patio table and dug through my purse for the car keys. I knew Justin had already left with Annie—I'd heard her car only minutes after they left our side. Where had they gone and how in the hell were they dealing with the demise of their relationship?

Frankie put his hand on the small of my back and walked me to the car. "I almost feel sorry for Sam. He has no connection to you anymore."

"Lucky him." Frankie was right, Sam was probably lucky to get out of this mess with no DNA connecting him to me.

"I'm the lucky one." Frankie was truly clueless. Yes, he had a new son. Yes, he was connected to me. But no, he was not lucky. In one night, twenty-five years ago, we created the brother of his lovely daughter. This did not feel like luck, more like, as Justin put it, one big clusterfuck.

"Yeah, real lucky, Frankie." My tone was rude, and I knew it. I shook my head and looked at him with sad eyes. Despite my sarcastic remark, he hugged me. He was a good man underneath it all.

****

Why wasn't Sam Justin's father? Would he be relieved to find out he was free of me and my son? Or, was he secretly hoping Justin was ours? As I turned the car south toward Sam's hotel, my heart began to race. He would have to wait a little longer. I needed to regroup, fix my makeup, comb my hair, change my clothes—this might be the last time I would ever see Sam—I wanted to look my best. The green machine seemed to know the way back to Sarah's house, taking me there on autopilot. When I saw Annie's car in the driveway, I wasn't surprised. The two of them probably had a lot to sort out to move from a romance to a brother-sister friendship.

As I opened the door, Justin was emerging from the kitchen with two of his favorite microbrews. Was he taking them out to the patio? He was heading the wrong direction for that. And why didn't he have his shirt on? His face was flushed, and his smile had returned, but as he looked at me, he seemed a bit sheepish. It was the look he gave me as a kid when he'd stolen a cookie from the cookie jar.

"What's going on, kiddo? Where's Annie?" Something wasn't right here.

"She's in my room, waiting for a beer."

"Really? Beer before noon? And what were you doing in your room? You did get the memo that she's your sister, right?" I was just standing there frozen, staring at my boy in disbelief. Did he think we were in Arkansas where it was legal to hook up with your first cousin? Even there, siblings were off-limits.

"Yeah, I got it." He was smiling from ear-to-ear now. "Frankie is my dad, but guess what? He's not Annie's biological dad."

"What? Why didn't Frankie tell us? What an ass!" I was fuming as I thought of Frankie just sitting there pretending to feel bad when Annie wasn't even his daughter. What reason could he have had to keep this from us? Now I understood their need for beer. Maybe I should have one, too.

"Don't be mad at Frankie, Mom. He doesn't know."

Annie emerged from the hallway. "Please don't say

anything to my dad, Mrs. Crandall." She moved toward Justin and took one of the beers. "I don't want him to ever know he's not my dad. That's what makes this complicated. I love your son, but I'm not sure we can go any further."

Justin put his arm around her. "I'm trying to convince her otherwise. He'll never know when we go back to San Francisco."

"But Justie, this isn't something we'll be able to keep secret. I want to be with you, but I don't want to break my dad's heart." She touched his face as she gazed into his loving eyes.

I was still standing there in a state of shock, my mouth hanging open, my eyes as wide as if I'd just seen a train wreck. Yeah, this was the closest thing I'd ever seen to a train wreck, the emotional carnage was mounting up quickly.

"What the hell is going on here? Please tell me who your father is and why Frankie was naïve enough to have thought you were his child. What did Marcia do?" That bitch. What had she done this time?

"My mom didn't do anything that bad. I know you and she aren't good friends, but she was, and is, a good mom. She was just afraid to tell my dad the truth."

"And exactly what is the truth?" I looked at Annie with her cornflower blue eyes—eyes that would not likely have come from an Italian father with ten generations of pure brown-eyed ancestors. I should have figured this out sooner.

As I moved toward Annie, Justin gently pushed me toward the kitchen table. It looked like we had a lot to talk about.

"My mom was engaged to my biological father. I

believe she really loved him and would have married him, but he died in a motorcycle accident." She took a sip of her beer. "At the funeral, she kept throwing up which everyone else attributed to grief, but I had a lot to do with it. She was pregnant with me."

"So why did Frankie think you were his?"

"You know my mom. She can be pretty tricky. She went crying to Dad on the day of the funeral and he was there to comfort her in her time of grief. I guess she made sure that comfort got him into bed with her and two weeks later she told him she was pregnant. The rest, as they say, is history."

"So why did Marcia tell you all this? Why didn't she want to keep it a secret from you, too?"

"I think she just had to tell someone, and when she and Dad got into one of their famous fights, she took me aside to assure me I was not related to him. What she didn't know is that I was devastated. I love my dad."

Looking at Annie, I finally understood. She was not like Frankie, or even Marcia for that matter. Her words were few but chosen carefully. Was that a product of her father's genes, or was she just unable to get a word in edgewise around Frankie and Marcia? I saw it as an understated strength. Yes, she was quiet, but not weak. She was a perfect match for my Justin.

I reached across the table and took Annie's hand. "Don't you think Frankie has a right to know?"

"It might change how he feels about me. I want him to believe I'm his little girl. This would kill him."

"I think you might be surprised. I can see how much he loves you and that's not because of biology. He loves all those memories of you growing up and how close the three of you were in those days. That was the happiest time of his life—he told me so."

"Mrs. Crandall…"

"Please call me Jamie." Or maybe she would call me "Mom" one of these days.

"Jamie, I just can't tell Dad. How would I even begin?" Her blue eyes appeared to be floating in a sea of tears, her long, dark lashes glistening. She would make me some beautiful grandchildren.

"You shouldn't tell him, and neither should I. Your mom needs to tell the truth. I think I'll pay her a visit."

Justin spoke up. "Mom, I usually hate it when you butt in and try to solve other people's problems, but this time I'm all for it."

"I'm not sure she'll listen to me, but it's worth a try." I reached toward my son. "Give me a swig of that beer, kid. I need some liquid courage."

Leaving the kids in the kitchen, I headed for the bathroom. I needed to fix my makeup and hair, not only for Sam, but for some reason I still had a need to impress Marcia. Why was I still so intimidated by this woman? I kept repeating my dad's favorite line, "Beauty is only skin deep" he would say to me, "but, ugly goes to the bone." It had given me comfort when I compared myself to her so many years ago. She was so beautiful—I wanted to believe that below that layer of exquisite skin there lived an ugly monster. Seeing her through Annie's eyes gave me new perspective. Now, instead of the monster that had grown to epic proportions in my mind, I saw Marcia as no more than a feisty puppy lashing out at anyone who came close to her secret. I could almost imagine the pain and guilt she must have felt, so now I was ready to approach her with kindness, not my usual accusation. She would never be my best friend again, but perhaps I could let go of some of the venom I'd been carrying around with me all these years.

Chapter Twenty-One
Marcia, Marcia, Marcia

I'd knocked on this door so many times when we were kids. It was odd that she had come full circle, living in her parents' house while they retired to Norway. That would be a perfect place for them—cold and full of evangelical Lutherans. No wonder Marcia had been a little wild in high school; she was rebelling from her strict religious roots. As a kid, I didn't understand all those family dynamics, but now it was starting to make sense.

And here I was knocking on that door again, remembering my best friend. Yes, Marcia had been my best friend from age five when she moved in next door to age twelve. Twelve was the magical age she realized I was not cool enough for her and her new BFF, Lisa Waltz. The truth was, I'd never been cool, but for seven years it hadn't mattered to Marcia. We'd been like two little dandelions, sunny and bright, but somewhere near the end of the seventh year she looked in the mirror and realized she had blossomed into an American Beauty Rose. I was still sunny and bright but hadn't evolved any further than maybe a daffodil. With Lisa by her side, Marcia's garden was now filled with nothing but roses, so she tossed me into the compost heap.

All this was happening the summer Frankie moved to our neighborhood. For some reason, he and I hit it off right away, and I believe I was his best friend. We shared secrets—he told me horror stories about his abusive past and me, well, I didn't really have any good secrets. Sensing my innocence, he did his best to push me off my straight and narrow path so I might have some secrets in my future. He taught me well.

So back then, I won his friendship, but Marcia won his heart. He'd been coming over to my backyard to talk to me, so he could catch a glimpse of Marcia on her deck next door. And while Frankie and I remained friends all through middle school, it was Marcia who wore his promise ring—at least for a little while. When she tired of the day-to-day coupledom, she'd break up with him. That happened every six months or so, giving her time to gather a troop of adoring boys. Whenever she saw him developing an interest in me, she wanted him back, and each time she got him back, she grew tired of him again. That went on for a while until eventually, Frankie's broken heart was handed to me. He was mine all through high school, but Marcia was always lurking in the background.

We had quite a history of sharing this man. I suppose he was a worthy prize, but the competition really was ridiculous. Did we want him, or did we just want to prove to the other that we were the better woman? I wondered as I waited for Marcia to answer the door.

The door opened, and there she was, beautiful as ever, her long blonde hair falling on her shoulders, her pink, sleeveless blouse bringing out the blush of her cheeks. Her blue eyes, so like Annie's, were not as bright as usual as they sank into puffy flesh. A black smudge on her cheek told me she'd been crying.

"Jamie? What are you doing here?"

"If you'll invite me in, I'll tell you?" I pulled the screen door my way, and she let me pass. We headed straight to the kitchen table where we'd spent so many hours of our youth.

"There's coffee in the pot, or maybe you want something stronger." I nodded that coffee would be fine as she prepared our cups. She continued. "I heard the news. Looks like Frankie has a son, something I could never give him."

"But you gave him a beautiful daughter, Marcia."

"Yeah, Annie is pretty great." Adding three teaspoons of sugar to her coffee, she kept her eyes on her cup, stirring and stirring and stirring. "I'm lucky to have her."

"Too bad she won't be able to stay with Justin, I mean, since they're related." I added some milk to my coffee and inhaled the aroma rising from the cup. "They're really in love, you know."

"Oh, I don't think they could have fallen in love so fast. They'll just have to move on." She was still stirring her coffee—the sound of the spoon scraping the porcelain was getting on my nerves.

"They don't want to move on, Marcia. And they wouldn't have to if you'd tell Frankie the truth about Annie." I heard the back door open. Was Annie home already?

"What do you mean? What is there to tell?" Her hands shook as she lifted the sweet coffee to her lips.

"You know what I'm talking about. Annie is not Frankie's daughter. If you tell him the truth, our kids will have a future."

Her eyebrows raised as she glared at me, my gaze

steady and strong—a standoff of sorts. Was she going to deny it again? Then she inhaled deeply, letting out a sigh as her breath released. She kept her eyes on me but softened her tone. "Jamie, I can't. It would hurt him too much. I can't do that to him."

"Since when do you care about hurting him? You're divorcing him, for God's sake."

"It's not because I don't love him." Her eyes dropped back to her coffee and away from her interrogator. "How did you know?"

"Annie told Justin, but I should have figured it out. Frankie comes from a long line of brown-eyed Italians. It would be surprising if he had any blue eye genes in his DNA. The biology doesn't add up."

"Do you think Frankie remembers his biology?" Her voice came to life as she spoke. "Do you think he's known all these years?"

"Lucky for you, I think Frankie flunked biology." I kept my voice calm—no longer feeling the need to lash out at Marcia—but firm. "You're probably safe, but you have to tell him, Marcia. This isn't about Frankie. It's about Justin and Annie."

Her eyes caught mine again, narrowing, she gave me that old look—the look that told me she had no use for me anymore. "Jamie, you just want me to embarrass myself, so you can have Frankie to yourself."

"I have to admit, I thought about that when I saw him Thursday night. But I can honestly say I don't have those feelings for him anymore." I returned her sour look, then smiled. "I suppose you won't want him now that I'm not interested."

Her eyes softened. "That's the funny thing, I do still want him. I think I needed you to come back to make me realize just how much. I can't believe how jealous I was when I saw you on the dance floor with my Frankie."

The old linoleum floor creaked over by the back door and Frankie stepped into the kitchen. Had he been standing in the shadows the whole time? I got my answer.

"You really still want me, Marcia?" She turned in her chair, and their eyes were locked on each other.

"I do, but I don't think you'll want me after what I've done. How much did you hear?"

"Enough." He kept his eyes on her. "Were you ever going to tell me the truth? If I hadn't walked in, would you have kept this secret another twenty-two years?"

"I would have. I didn't ever want you to think Annie was not your child."

"She is my child. I don't care what the DNA says, she's my daughter. This doesn't change my love for her." He crossed the room and pulled Marcia from her chair. Grabbing her shoulders, he begged her for an answer. "Why didn't you tell me? Why?"

She tried to look away, but he lifted her chin, forcing her to look at him. "I couldn't. I was ashamed of tricking you into marrying me. I was still grieving over Cameron—I just wanted you to take care of me. If I'd told you the truth, I thought you'd leave me, and I didn't want to raise Annie alone."

"I'm not stupid. I think I knew I was second choice, but when you got pregnant, I thought that might change things."

She reached up and touched his face. "It did, but not the way I expected. When Annie was born and I saw how you looked at her, I fell in love with you—

really in love with you—for the first time."

"That was an amazing day, seeing a new life come into the world—our Annie." He wrapped his arms around her. "We raised a beautiful girl. But how will she feel when she finds out I'm not her biological father?"

"She knows. I told her five years ago, after you and I had a fight."

"Why didn't she say anything?"

"She said she didn't want things to change—she wanted you to love her as your own."

"Nothing could change the way I feel about Annie." He looked at Marcia so tenderly. "And nothing will change the way I feel about you, Marcia. I love you." He brought his hands to her cheeks, and then he kissed her.

I had been right about his feelings for Marcia, but I had been so wrong about Marcia. She had a good heart. It had been a little uncomfortable watching their exchange, but I learned a lot about both of them. They loved their daughter and, clearly, they still loved each other.

I waved as I let myself out the front door. We would tell Justin and Annie tonight, but it looked like Frankie and Marcia had other things on their mind now.

Chapter Twenty-Two
Telling Sam

Frankie and Marcia didn't hear me leave. They were too busy making googly eyes at each other to notice little insignificant Jamie slip out the front door. Was that the same Frankie who wanted me so desperately only two hours earlier? He was a strange guy, so willing to move from Marcia to me, but was he really? It was high school all over again—I was the rebound—and looking back I wondered if I had always been second choice. To see those two now, it was clear they belonged together.

As I drove toward the freeway, I glanced in the rearview mirror taking in my old neighborhood one last time, then moved my tired eyes to face the road ahead of me. This road would lead me to Sam, the man who had loved me so long—the man who had finally given up. Remembering the day I met him in seventh grade, I could almost feel his eyes on me. He sat across the aisle and while I was listening intently to Mrs. Miller enthusiastically explain the overuse of adverbs, I felt some blue heat coming from my left side. When I looked over, there was Sam, his sky-blue eyes boring into me like laser beams. Apparently, he had a thing for studious girls with black-rimmed glasses. At first glance, I thought he might be cute under his own thick glasses, but the pocket protector in his shirt, which was buttoned up to his Adam's apple, told me he was too nerdy...even for me. I rejected his advances, holding out for Frankie to come to his senses. While I was waiting for my bad boy, Sam and I settled into a comfortable friendship that fed my brain. What I didn't notice then was it fed my soul as well.

As the years passed from seventh grade through high school, Sam had evolved—the pocket protector was long gone, and the top button was rarely buttoned—but I hadn't seen the evolution. I continued to see the brainy, young boy, refusing to believe he could possibly be capable of romance. Prince Charming was not supposed to wear glasses and carry a calculator. Now, twenty-five years later, I started adding up his virtues. I was the one who needed a calculator to count the ways I had grown to love Sam Bradley. I loved everything about him, from his offbeat sense of humor to his tender touch, sweet kiss...and so much more. Yes, I loved Sam, and I hoped with all my heart that he would give me a second chance.

Two days ago, I walked into the lobby of the Edgewater, and there was my Sam, smiling and looking so hot in his khaki shorts. Today, there was no Sam to greet me. I stood alone staring at the silver door of the elevator. Would it ever open? I took a deep breath—I think I'd forgotten to breathe on the way to the hotel—inhaling the aroma of coffee and grilled salmon as it drifted from the restaurant to the lobby. Having always loved seafood, I was surprised that I gagged at the smell, feeling gratitude when my ride to the third floor finally arrived. As I stepped out of the elevator, the subtle scent of saltwater set my mind wandering to Sam's kiss on the beach only a few nights ago. Room three hundred and three was a short walk down the hallway—it should have been easy—if only my legs didn't feel like limp noodles. Despite the heat of another sweltering day, my body shivered as I lifted my hand to knock. Before my fist touched the door, it opened. Sam stood there with one bag over his shoulder and another rolling behind him.

"Jamie!" He smiled, by accident I think, then the serious look I had seen on Saturday night returned to his face. "What are you doing here? I've been waiting to hear from you, but I didn't think you'd come in person."

"I had to see you again, Sam. Will you let me in?" I stumbled and he dropped his bag to take my arm.

"Come sit down, Jamie. You look terrible. Does that mean you have bad news for me?" He led me to the king-sized bed where we both sat facing the water. I turned toward him.

"It depends on what you consider bad news—being a father or being deprived of that gift." I searched his eyes wondering which outcome he hoped for. "If you wanted to be a father, it *is* bad news, but if you want to be free of me, it's good news. You're not Justin's dad."

I watched the tears form in his eyes, pain drawing its sharp lines on his brow. Then he put his head in his hands and sobbed. In all the years I'd known Sam, I had never seen him cry. He was always in control, stoic in his emotions—or should I say lack of them. But now he cried uncontrollably. This was not the boy I had known in high school. This was the man I wanted to know now.

I wrapped my arm around him, resting my hand on the back of his neck. "Are you okay?"

His words were barely audible as he caught his breath. "Not really." He lifted his head from his hands and his eyes burned a hole in my heart. "I've always wanted to be a father—a better father than the one I had. As hard as it might have been to become a father to a twenty-four-year-old, I was hoping I'd get a chance."

"It wouldn't have been hard. Justin is easy to love. But you probably wouldn't have forgiven me for taking those twenty-four years from you."

"I don't know. Maybe. Maybe not. But it's a moot point—I'm not a dad—that's the final blow." He brought his hand to my face, his touch surprisingly soft. "I'd given up on that dream and as angry as I was that you'd kept this from me, I secretly hoped Justin was my son." Then the realization hit him. "God, he and Annie must be devastated. It would have been better for all of us if I was his father."

"I agree, it would have been better for Justin to have you in his life, but it turns out Annie isn't Frankie's biological daughter—long story."

"Well, at least there's some good news."

"Good for Justin, but not for you. I'm so sorry, Sam. I really made a mess of things." I stroked the hair on the back of his neck. "I wish there was something I could do to make things better."

"It's okay, Jamie." He reached across me to the bedside table to pull a tissue from the box. "I shouldn't have gotten so mad, especially since Justin isn't my son." He blew his nose. "Now you and Frankie can be together—you seem to have a special bond, and this makes it even stronger. I guess that's the reason I exploded when Marcia told me about the DNA testing.

You lied to me—I just couldn't believe it. And then I looked at you wrapped in Frankie's arms. I finally came to my senses."

"And when you told me it was over, I finally came to *my* senses." I touched his tear-stained face. "You have always been there for me. You were my best friend. I want to pick up where we left off, although the friendship doesn't feel quite the same as it did twenty-five years ago. You still make me laugh—and you make me think. We're never at a loss for words. But the thing that made me realize that you were the one was the butterflies in my stomach. When I get a whiff of your spicy scent, my head starts spinning, my stomach feels that flutter." I couldn't tell Sam, but that was the way I felt when I met Paul. That was the sign I had been ignoring all week. Love does come knocking more than once in a lifetime, but would Sam give me another chance?

"You know how I feel about you, Jamie. Even your deception can't erase all the good feelings, but after the dishonesty in my marriage, my knee-jerk reaction is to run away."

"Please don't. I love you, Sam." He had to see the truth in those words when he looked in my eyes.

"I've wanted to hear those words for so many years. I wish I could just take you in my arms and say everything will be okay." Surely, he could see how I felt. Would he change his mind? "But I feel so empty right now. Still no child and how do I know you won't run back to Frankie?"

"Because I went to great lengths to get Frankie and Marcia back together. I can't believe I'm saying this, but she seems to have some redeeming qualities. After watching them, I think they belong together."

"And you're not sorry about that?"

"Not at all. I admit it. He was the one I wanted when I was seventeen, but we're not in high school anymore. The roles have reversed, Mr. Bradley."

"You know, I think I believe you, but now I'm the one who needs some time." His face, with a furrowed brow and searching eyes, told me he forgave me. At least I would have that last memory. "I have a flight to catch, so I need to get moving. I really didn't think you'd come in person after the other night."

"I'll let you go, but I won't give up. I really do love you, Sam."

"I love you, too, Jamie." He hugged me so tight I could barely breathe. I felt his body shake with a new round of sobs—or was that my body? We were both crying and clinging to one another, but it was definitely goodbye. He let me go and reached for his bags. "You can stay here for a while if you'd like."

"I think I will." I sat on the unmade bed and watched him walk out the door. The unmade bed—Sam was not as rigid as I thought. I looked around and saw an open drawer and an empty bottle. He was human. He was not so perfect, and he had discovered that I was not so perfect either. God, I hoped he would give me another chance.

I looked out the window at the nearly waveless Sound. The water was so smooth—such a contrast to all our lives this week. What could have been a tidal wave had transitioned into a merely choppy sea that seemed to be settling for everyone. Justin could continue his pursuit of Annie, Frankie and Marcia were reconciling, and Dad and I were back on good terms. Sarah's sunny optimism had been well-founded. Everything had worked out just fine. Well, almost everything.

I laid on the bed and inhaled the scent on the sheets—a mix of Old Spice and Sam's sweat. I pulled them up to my chin and took in a long deep breath. Exhaustion took over as I fell into a deep sleep, dreaming of my Sam coming back to me. I felt a hand on my shoulder. Was he really coming back?

No, not today. It was the maid touching my shoulder, telling me it was way past checkout time.

Chapter Twenty-Three
No More Secrets

I walked to my car in a daze, still groggy from my two-hour nap in Sam's bed. The good old green Fiesta was a welcome sight—my getaway car—there to take me back to Sarah's cheery, yellow home. I wasn't sure the bright décor, or even Sarah, could cheer me up right now, but at least I would be back where I felt safe and secure.

With rush hour traffic, I inched my way to the freeway, sucking exhaust fumes in through the open window. Had I pushed the power window button too hard? Was the button locked in the childproof mode? I didn't know what I'd done, but I couldn't shut the damn window, and now I couldn't breathe. By the time I merged from Mercer Street onto the northbound lanes of I-5, I was about to pass out from holding my breath. The only thing worse than the exhaust was my exhaustion. The fumes and warm wind in my hair managed to keep me alert enough to get me to Sarah's driveway. Finally "home," I forced my tired body to take those last few steps to the front door.

I looked at my watch—five fifty p.m.—our childhood dinner hour. Mom wouldn't be cooking tonight, and Dad's jaunty step was absent. That time didn't mean what it once had, but it triggered so many memories. Now it was merely a number—five fifty—

but as I arrived at my sister's home, I was hoping for the kind of comfort I felt as a child.

"Look what the cat dragged in," Sarah said as she opened the door. Her eyes caught mine, then drifted down to Delilah who was sitting on the porch with a mouse in her mouth, the long tail brushing my ankle. Was she talking about the mouse or me? Although my face was gray, I'd been anything but mousy today.

"Hey, watch your mouth, Sarah." I stepped away from the hunter and her prey as Sarah forced Delilah to drop her gift at the front door. "I know I look like shit. You don't have to rub it in."

"Sorry, Jamie, I wasn't really referring to how you looked. Where have you been all this time?"

"Everywhere—Frankie's house, Marcia's house, Sam's hotel." I started to cry again.

"Come here, Sis." Sarah grabbed me in a tight hug. When she finally let go, she led me to the kitchen table where last night's leftovers were on the table. "You must be hungry. I already ate, and David is having dinner with some of his coworkers tonight, so this is all yours."

No wonder I was so exhausted. I hadn't had a thing to eat since breakfast—I needed some fuel. "I'm ravenous. And I hope that's coffee I smell—I could really use some caffeine."

Sarah poured me a cup of coffee, and I scarfed down potato salad, beans, and some reheated ribs. The juice dripped down my chin as I began talking with my mouth full. "Did you talk to Justin and Annie?"

"Yeah, they told me the whole story. They were kind of surprised you didn't call after your meeting with Marcia."

"Oh, damn, I was going to call them when I got to Sam's hotel, but I wasn't thinking straight. I take it Frankie called to tell them Marcia came clean." I took a big gulp of coffee. "I hope Annie isn't too mad at Marcia."

"What? You're worried about Marcia's feelings?"

"Weird, isn't it? I kind of feel sorry for her. I really hope she and Frankie can make things work this time."

"Wow!" Sarah put her hand on my forehead. "Who are you, and what have you done with my sister?"

"I guess I'm past that high school rivalry. I don't want to fight her anymore."

"Are you just tired of fighting, or are you finally through with Frankie?"

"I'm through. I know Sam's the one I love."

"And how did he take the paternity news?"

"Not well. I think he wanted to be a dad. He's pretty hurt by this whole thing. His pride might just keep him away forever."

"Well, if he can't loosen up a bit and come to his senses, it's his loss."

"It's not like I broke his favorite coffee mug. This was pretty big. I kept this secret from him for twenty-five years. I can't really blame him for holding on to his anger for a while."

"I'm so sorry, honey. Is there anything good you can take from this?"

I smiled for the first time today. "Oh, yes!" I reached across the table and took Sarah's hands. "Justin is happy, and I have Dad back in my life. That would be enough, but there's more. I don't have to hide anymore. I didn't know how this would affect everyone's lives, but we all survived." I squeezed her hands. "And now, I have no more secrets!"

"Jamie, I'm so proud of you. You made it through this, and even if Sam doesn't wake up, at least you know you can love again. Maybe there is someone out there who will be even better than Sam."

"There's no one better than Sam," I said quietly. I let go of Sarah and put my hands back in my lap. "He loved me for twenty-five years—I'll give him six months. I know he still loves me."

"I hope he doesn't disappoint you. You know, Jamie, I'm glad you're ready to live again, but you don't have to fall in love with the first guy you have sex with after your five-year drought. Besides, he seems kind of unforgiving."

"I don't think he's unforgiving—he's hurt, and he's not sure he can trust me. He's played second fiddle to Frankie all these years, and I don't think he can quite believe I'm really in love with him."

"Are you sure you really are in love with him?"

"I'm sure." I felt a calm resolve as I smiled at my sister. "Tell me, Sarah, how did you know David was 'the one'?"

"I didn't, at least not at first. He was definitely the cutest guy in my chemistry class, and he kept asking me out, but I just couldn't see myself with some nerdy scientist. I was still in my wild phase back then and was in no mood to be tamed."

"What changed?"

"He asked me if I wanted to study with him. He was a genius, and I was struggling with the material, so I decided to take advantage of his brain. What harm could it do?"

"So, you were using him?" I laughed for the first

time today.

"Yeah. I'm not proud of it now, but I really needed the help—and he helped me understand and enjoy the sciences enough to change my focus."

"Was that when you fell for him?"

"No, I was starting to like him, though. He didn't seem quite as stiff as I was expecting." She smiled as her eyes glazed over and looked right through me. Was she imagining the moment? She refocused her eyes on me. "It was a week later when I reluctantly agreed to a date—it was the least I could do after he helped me pass my final. He took me to the zoo where I learned he loved animals, and as we stood in front of the lion's den, he kissed me. That was it for me—I felt that kiss through my entire body. We always joke about him taming his wild lioness in front of the lion's den."

"Were you ever worried your differences would be a problem?"

"Never. That day I decided I'd do whatever it took to hold on to this guy. I'd change if I had to, but guess what? He liked me just the way I was. I didn't have to change, and he didn't either. We fit surprisingly well."

"And after twenty-three years you two are better than ever. I'm so glad life worked out so well for you two." I stood up and walked around the table. "I'm sorry to leave you here alone, but I need to go lay down. It's pretty early to go to bed, but I'm really beat." Sarah stood up, and we shared a warm hug. I clung to her as I laid my head on her shoulder. "I love you, Sis."

"Love you, too. Sleep well."

I brushed my teeth but didn't bother to wash off my makeup. It seemed redundant—the tears had done a good job of removing almost every trace of color I'd applied to my face this morning. I crawled into bed and softly fluffed the three pillows behind me. There was no need to beat them up tonight. Leaning into the soft, yellow satin I reached for my phone.

Should I or shouldn't I send Sam a text? What the hell—what did I have to lose? I had no idea when his plane was getting in, but he'd left me at three p.m. and it was almost eight p.m. now. I typed the words: — *Please text when you're home safe*— I waited a few minutes—no answer. Either he was still on the plane or driving home—or ignoring me. I had to let it go.

The man I needed to talk to was not Sam. I tapped the screen on my phone, remembering the number that hadn't changed in forty-two years.

"Hello?" That was the voice I wanted to hear.

"Hi, Dad."

"Hi, sweetie. I've been thinking about you all day. How did things turn out?"

"Not as bad as I was expecting, but not as good as I hoped."

I told him the whole story, every detail from the devastation of the morning to the ensuing revelation, reconciliation, and celebrations. I didn't give him the details of Justin and Annie's beer-enhanced celebration in the bedroom, but I'm sure he got the picture. He sounded happy for Frankie—they had become friends over the years—and he didn't seem to have the same vitriol for Marcia that I had carried around all these years. We laughed about Frankie's journey with that woman, Dad comparing her to his own complicated wife. Mom and Marcia were a bit alike—beautiful, but difficult.

I ended the story as I had ended the day, mourning

the end of my relationship with Sam. Dad tried to find words to soothe my pain.

"That damn Sam. I always liked that kid, too. You and 'Little Sammy Wonder' were a cute couple."

"Oh, Dad, we were never a couple, just good friends."

"That's what it takes for a good relationship, sweetie. You've got to be friends. I used to watch you two study together, laughing and goofing around. I wondered why you chose Frankie instead of the guy who fit you so perfectly."

"Well, I finally figured it out, but it's too late."

"As long as you're still breathing, it's not too late. He may come around."

"I'm not counting on it. But Dad, there's one thing I am counting on. I need to spend the day with you at the Pike Place Market. I always loved going there, and when Sarah and David talked about it the other day, it brought back so many memories. Let's get Justin and Annie to go with us. Are you free on Wednesday?"

"I'm retired. I'm always free." I could almost hear his smile over the phone.

"Good, let's do it. Wednesday at eleven. We'll pick you up in our green machine."

"You can park that piece of crap here, but I'll drive." We laughed and said our goodbyes, and I put the phone on the night table.

It was only eight thirty p.m., but I was exhausted. I turned out the light and curled into the fetal position, sinking into the soft pillows. As I started to drift off, I heard the tritone ding of my phone. I reached over and read the text from Sam:—*I'm home*— Not much, but it was something.

Chapter Twenty-Four
Farewell Seattle

Where had Tuesday gone? After ten hours of deep, dead to the world, sleep I rose from my trance and joined Sarah for a muffin and coffee. As soon as she left for work, I stumbled back down the hallway, allowing myself four more glorious hours of healing slumber. God, I was tired, but the sound of the key in the front door and the fact that I just couldn't sleep another minute got me out of bed—at least for a few hours. The key was Justin's. Returning from a night with Annie, he had just come home to shower and change clothes. Good for him—he seemed happier than I'd seen him in five years. Although he didn't have much time for me, he promised that he and Annie would join Dad and me at the Pike Place Market the next day.

After Justin left, I took my book out to the back deck, found a shady spot for the chaise lounge, and laid there all day reading and dozing. It had been a lazy day with very little human contact—just what I needed after days of confronting all the major players from my past.

I could sum up Tuesday in a series of "No's:" No more secrets to reveal. No more rivals to confront. No more ex-boyfriends to face. No more apologies to my son. No more second-guessing my father. No more conflict—that was nice. Every "No" was indeed a positive turn in my life—every "No" except one—No more Sam.

Throughout the day, I cried, I read, I dozed, then I ate a quiet dinner with Sarah and David and went back to bed. It was a cleansing day, and peace came over me as I fell asleep, anticipating tomorrow with Dad and the kids.

****

Twenty-five years was too long between visits to the Pike Place Market. I couldn't wait to immerse myself in the heart of Seattle with the men I loved most. And it would be nice to get to know Annie—I had a feeling she was well on her way to becoming a permanent part of our family.

"Hey, Mom, are you up?" Justin called through my door. I was up and had already showered, dried my hair, and applied enough makeup to look presentable.

"I'm ready." I opened my door to see Justin and Annie smiling—no, glowing—with the light of new love. "Let's get this show on the road," I said, remembering those words from the many times my dad used them to usher his family out the door.

"You look tired, Mom."

"I'm actually so rested I probably won't be able to sleep for days. I think I slept eighteen of the last twenty-four hours, if you count all my naps." I glanced at my reflection in the hallway mirror. He was right. The bags under my eyes were pronounced. "I'm really starting to feel better than I did on Monday. That was a hell of a day."

"It's over now, Mom. You can relax." He wrapped his arm around my shoulder. "And I can't thank you enough for talking to Marcia. You rock, Mom."

"Thanks, kiddo. I'm glad it's working out for you two."

Annie looked at me and smiled. "Things couldn't be better. You raised an awesome son."

Justin's cheeks turned pink as he spoke to her. "And Frankie raised an awesome daughter." They looked at one another with that syrupy, sweet look of new love. If he weren't my own son, the syrup would have made me nauseous.

"Okay you lovebirds, let's get out of here." I reached in my purse for the keys, and we headed out the door and into the Fiesta. It was time to take that car literally and have our own little Fiesta. I turned up the volume on the radio and forced them—well, strongly encouraged them—to sing along with AC/DC's "Highway to Hell" on the oldies station. I'm not sure Annie knew all the words, but Justin had been schooled in old rock n' roll by Paul, and my son didn't miss a beat. Contrary to the song, we had escaped Hell and were on the path to a brighter future—I was starting to feel tingling waves of life-affirming joy course through my tired body. Even the next song by the Rolling Stones, "You Can't Always Get What You Want," was not going to bring me down. And as the song ended, reminding me "you just might find, you get what you need," we arrived at Dad's house. I needed this day with Dad.

He was watching out the window, and as I parked across the street, the garage door rose to reveal Dad's red car. I can't remember a time when our family didn't have a red car, usually a Buick, a good, sturdy vehicle. Dad had stuck to the red, but this was definitely not a Buick. He walked out of the garage, beaming.

"Like my new wheels?"

"Oh my God!!" I couldn't believe my eyes—a ruby red Mustang convertible. "When did you get this?"

"Yesterday." His chest was puffed out and his eyes were wide with delight. "If I see one more goddamn Buick, I think I'll puke."

"And I was so looking forward to a nice steady ride in the old Buick," I laughed.

"Hey, Grandpa, this is awesome." Justin put his arm around Dad and hugged him. "I knew you'd be cool." He reached for Annie's hand. "And speaking of cool, Grandpa, this is Annie."

"Oh, I know Annie. I've known her since she was a toddler when Frankie and Marcia moved back to the neighborhood." He hugged her. "Glad to see you found yourself a nice boy, Annie." They both laughed as they exchanged a "look."

"Thanks, Grandpa Jack." She gave him a wink. "Nice car—I had a feeling the Buicks weren't your idea."

"Smart girl. I think you should keep her, Justin."

Justin shook his head, obviously surprised by Annie's close relationship with his grandpa. "Don't worry, I'm never letting this girl getaway."

The threads that connected us were almost tangible. When Frankie moved to this neighborhood thirty years ago, we had no way of knowing that all our lives would change—or be created—because of him. If his father hadn't abused his mother, or if his mother hadn't had the sense to send him to a safer home, we would not all be standing here today. Life was pretty damn precarious. Each decision to zig instead of zag, changed the entire order of things. If Frankie's father hadn't been a jerk, our paths would never have crossed. But they did cross and in spite of—or probably because of—the roller-coaster ride Frankie and I called a relationship, things worked out for the best. Justin was the product of our mistake. But now I saw that it wasn't a mistake at all.

Dad put his arm around me. "You're a million miles away, Jamie. Are you okay?"

"I'm great, Dad." I felt a lump growing in my throat. "I'm so happy to have you back in my life. I never thought I'd see this day." Wrapping my arms around his neck, I hugged him as tight as I had the day I left home. That was a day of parting—today was a day to celebrate our decision to come together. "I love you, Dad."

"I love you, too, sweetie." He gave my shoulder a reassuring squeeze.

I loosened my grip. I didn't have to hold so tight—he wasn't going anywhere. But now I was ready to get going back to one of my favorite childhood destinations. "Let's get into this Mustang and hit the road."

Dad opened the passenger door. Ah, that new car smell—the smell and the rich look of the black leather was powerful. The stale scent of Dad's cigars and Mom's perfume in the old Buick was being replaced with the invigorating aroma of the Mustang. It was time for Dad to gallop into the future in this ruby red stallion.

Justin raced past me, ushering Annie into the back seat, then following close behind. Dad started the mechanism to lower the roof, and as soon he and I got in and buckled up, he turned the ignition, revealing the purr of this pony's magnificent engine. We were off!

We barely spoke as we drove downtown, partly because we couldn't hear over the open-air ride through traffic, but mostly because we were all enjoying the rush of wind in our hair. Traveling in the convertible went to our heads, seemingly elevating our status from stodgy Buick people to parade-worthy royalty. As we passed lesser vehicles, I resisted the impulse to wave and flaunt our good fortune.

"We're here!" Dad announced as he parked on the corner of First and Pike—not the safest place in town. He topped off the car with a push of the button, and we were on our way to the market.

Inhaling the salty sea air mixed with the aroma of baked goods, fruits, vegetables, and fresh fish, memories of childhood filled my head. I literally started skipping down the street. "God, I love this place."

"I get that you like the Market, Mom, but do you really have to skip?"

"Am I embarrassing you, kiddo? Are you too grown up to act a little goofy?"

"Yes, and yes." Holding Annie's hand, he walked calmly a few feet behind me.

"I'm not too old." Dad said it as he skipped—or tried to skip—to catch up to me. He grabbed my hand, just as he had when I was a child, and we ran down the hill toward the big clock at the entrance to the market. It looked so much like the market of my childhood, but I immediately spied a new addition.

"What an adorable bronze pig," I mused.

"That's Rachel. She's a piggy bank, collecting for the food bank, senior center, childcare center, and medical clinic in the Market." Dad reached in his pocket for change, and I dug through my purse, pulling out a dollar to add to the bank.

"I'm still unemployed," Annie spoke in an apologetic voice.

"I got ya covered." Justin pulled out a five-dollar bill and added it to Rachel's collection. My son was the big money earner of the group, earning six figures at the tender age of twenty-four. A Stanford education, a mathematical mind, and encouraging parents propelled my son—a boy with a purpose—to his goal as a software designer. I was so proud of him.

Annie was aware of her good fortune in finding a man like Justin. I could see it in her cornflower blue eyes. But my son saw her as the prize. They walked arm in arm, his hand stroking her long, dark hair. Annie turned her head to make sure Dad and I were following.

"C'mon, Grandpa Jack, let's show Justin and Jamie the fish guys. Watching them toss those salmon is almost like watching a Seahawks game."

"I wouldn't go that far." Dad tugged at the bill of his favorite Seahawks cap. "Annie, you're moving to enemy territory in San Francisco. I hope these two Bay Area residents aren't going to change your allegiance."

"Not a chance." She gave Justin a big smile and he just glared back.

"Is this going to be our first fight?" Justin asked.

I chimed in. "Don't worry, Dad. You raised me to be a Seahawk supporter and I never became a 49er fan. Paul and I had some words about that, but Justin is another story. He was born and raised there." I still remembered my high school years, going to Seahawks games with Dad. I loved my son, but sometimes questioned his allegiance to those damn 49ers.

When we arrived at the fish market, the guys were indeed tossing fish and putting on a show. How this ever became a world-famous activity was beyond me, but I had to admit it was fun to watch.

As we explored the produce stalls, I chose to buy fruit from the older men and women who had obviously been bringing their goods to the market since I was a child. This was their livelihood, and it did my heart good to support their life's work. I wondered if they would survive the market refurbishment that was underway. The old wooden walkways and rustic stalls would likely not survive—I was glad I came back when I did, so I could see the market as it had been twenty-five years ago.

"Hey, Mom, Annie and I were thinking about walking down to the Big Wheel. Do you want to come with us?"

"I was just there the other day with Sam." My eyes filled with tears. "I don't think I could handle it."

Justin came over to me immediately. "Please don't be sad, Mom. I'm sorry about you and Sam." He hugged me. "This is probably pretty bad timing, but can you give me Sam's number?"

"Why would you want his number?"

"His company is a subsidiary of Cupertino. I think we could help each other."

"Oh, okay." I recited the number and Justin typed it into his phone. "Now you kids go play on that Big Wheel. It is pretty awesome."

Dad and I continued our trek, traveling to the lower levels of the market. There we found a treasure in a little specialty bookstore—a used copy of *101 Famous Poems*. If it weren't for Dad, I may not have developed a love of poetry, or books for that matter. His nightly recitals of the poems in this book turned my choice of a major in college from Economics—Mom's suggestion—to English. Mom was probably just as mad about my choice of English over Economics as she was about the pregnancy. I smiled thinking about that fateful choice.

"What's with the silly grin?" Dad caught up with me just as I found the book. "I just found your favorite book." Opening it, I found the line that had gotten me through the last five years and would hopefully get me through the next five. I read it aloud. "*I am the master of my fate; I am the captain of my soul.*"

"Yes, you are, sweetie." He gently took the book from me as we walked toward the clerk. "Let this be my gift to you for giving me a second chance."

Two hours later, after meeting the kids for lunch at Kells Irish Pub, we made our way back to the red stallion, lowered the convertible top, and headed to Dad's house. He invited us in for a beer or lemonade, and we topped the day off on the patio—the same patio on which Dad and I shared harsh words only a week ago. This felt better, but I had to admit it felt kind of empty without Mom.

"Dad, I think I told you Sam's parents split up. You know, his mom is a really nice woman."

"And your point is?" He took a sip of his favorite Heineken beer as I sipped my lemonade.

"Well, you're still a young man at sixty-seven. Maybe you should get back in the game."

Justin jumped on it. "Yeah, Grandpa, go for it." Annie nodded her approval.

"I think I'm better off without a woman in my life.

It was a rough forty-five years with your grandma."

I could relate to that, even though I'd only had seventeen years with her. "Maybe the next forty-five will be better with the right woman. It can't hurt to meet someone new. Let me give you Sam's number. You can ask him what he thinks."

He smiled a gentle, almost shy, smile. "I guess it couldn't hurt."

When we finished our drinks, we said our goodbyes. I knew it would be a while before I saw Dad again, but I also knew I'd be talking to him at least once a week from now on. The last thing he said to me as we walked to the car—the look in his brown eyes, the tone of his voice, the quiver of his chin as he spoke—will live inside my head forever.

"I love you, sweetie." What more could I ask?

****

That night I slept better than I'd slept in years. The burden of the past twenty-five years had felt like a backpack full of concrete, but now the backpack seemed to be filled with feathers. Nothing I couldn't carry.

And the next day my load was lightened further when Jody Rose came by. She forgave me for the twenty-five-year cold shoulder and was willing to start fresh. Jennifer Brown was not so forgiving, especially when she heard Frankie was back with Marcia. In time, her new interest in Gary Daniels might heal the wound, but I wasn't going to hold my breath. Julie was probably the most upset after she witnessed the emotional carnage between Sam and me. Apparently, after I left the reunion, she tried all evening to rescue him from my clutches, but Jody told me he wasn't having any of it. Although he wasn't physically in my clutches, he clearly was not moving on. Jody's words gave me a small ray of hope. Of all my female friends from high school, Jody was the one with the kindest heart. It was great to have her back in my life.

My last day in Seattle, Friday, was spent packing and pondering my future. I was feeling sick again. Damn it! All my past mistakes had been revealed and now I should be able to relax, but this tired, sick feeling left me with one more secret. Was I dying? It sure felt like it, but Sarah convinced me I would live through this. Telling Justin and Annie could wait—they were so happy; I didn't want to put a damper on their euphoria. I would see my doctor when I got home to confirm what I already knew and start treatment.

Chapter Twenty-Five
Going Home

If anyone had told me ten days would change my life, I would have laughed in their face, but now I knew ten days had indeed changed everything—mostly for the good. As I watched Justin and Annie board the plane in front of me, I was grateful for the serendipitous combination of eggs and seeds that created these two beautiful kids, allowing them to stay together. There was nothing I wouldn't do for my son, and orchestrating Marcia's confession not only saved our children's relationship, it healed her marriage. Healing my heart was an unexpected by-product of our long-overdue encounter.

"Let me put your bag up, Mom." I hadn't even had to carry it past the third row.

"Thanks, kiddo, and thanks for upgrading us to first class. It's nice having rich relatives." He was so generous with his good fortune. He would save for his future, but he would never be stingy.

"You reap what you sow," Justin said. He had learned that from me. For many years, I had little to give, but I always told him to give what he could to others. He learned that lesson well.

"Well, I'm happy to reap the benefits of your generosity. This extra room will make a nice resting place." I sat across the aisle from them, hoping the seat next to me would remain empty. I just wanted to relax and read the poetry book Dad had given me at the market.

Settling in, I stared out the window, watching the cargo handlers load our larger bags onto the plane—all there, thankfully. Passengers continued to file past us until the plane was nearly full and still no one claimed the seat beside me. I jumped when I heard the tritone ding, reminding me I needed to turn my phone to airplane mode. Who would be sending me a text message? Everyone knew I was flying home today. I looked down—I couldn't believe my eyes. It was from Sam.

Sam: —*I love you, Jamie. Will you give me a second chance?*—

Me: —*Yes!! I love you, too. When will I see you?*—

My heart felt like it would burst. I leaned across the aisle and tapped Justin's shoulder. He and Annie both looked over. "Sam just texted me."

"Really? Are you going to see him?" Justin said as a matter of fact. I guess guys don't get as excited about these things. Annie smiled, sharing my joy.

"You better believe it. I just don't know where and when." I had to lean back. I thought all the passengers had already boarded, but some guy was entering the aisle. I moved my head back to let the man pass.

"How about here and now." I looked up. It was Sam! Justin and Annie were both smiling now—they knew—as Sam slid into the seat next to me. His strong hands cupped my face, his blue eyes capturing mine as he kissed me. I closed my disbelieving eyes to accept the soft, tender touch of his lips—so soft at first, then growing with the same hunger I had been feeling since we parted. Was I dreaming? Was he really here? I pulled away, out of breath, and lost myself in his gaze. Yes, this was real.

"What made you change your mind?" He stroked my hair, brushing a stray lock off my cheek. "I almost changed my mind when you came to me at the Edgewater. I think I knew you were sincere, but I just couldn't let go of my foolish pride. I felt betrayed, and I wasn't going to be put in that position again."

"And now?" I touched his bare knee—he was wearing those khaki shorts again so I should have recognized his cute legs walking down the aisle. "You said you *almost* changed your mind."

"Well, you know me, I gave it a lot of thought—analyzed it to death, actually. Then I got a little unsolicited help from your friends and family."

"What? What kind of help? And who?"

"Sarah called on Tuesday. I'm not sure she even likes me—she was kind of short with me. I guess she was just being protective of you. She told me you were miserable without me and maybe I should do something about that." He moved his hand from my hair to my shoulder and gently down my arm. He wrapped his warm fingers around my much colder hand.

"So Sarah convinced you to come here?"

"Not, totally. She convinced me to call you when you got home, but then I got a text from Justin. After a few texts, I called him, and we had quite a long talk. That boy loves you so much, Jamie."

I looked across the aisle at my son, his grin as wide as the Grand Canyon. "I know." I blushed.

"After talking to him, my wall of pride started to break down. I knew I wanted to see you, but you know how hard it is for me to back down once I've made a decision."

"But my boy got you thinking?"

"He did. I could learn a lot about love and forgiveness from him. I wish he were my son. He's a great kid."

"You don't have to convince me of that. But that was Wednesday, and today is Saturday. When did you decide to come sweep me off my feet?"

"It only took two more people to tell me how stupid I was to let you go." He laughed a little too loudly. I couldn't help giggling over his admission.

"And who were those two people?"

"Well, one was a friend of mine and yours, Jody Rose. She told me in no uncertain terms that I better get my ass up to Seattle and claim my prize—you! Apparently, she's been hoping we'd get together since high school. She told me she really believed you wanted me and only me."

"That's true." I squeezed his hand. "So that's when you booked your flight up here?"

"No, it was three hours later, after I talked to your dad."

"He called you, too?"

"He did. And when he broke down and cried, telling me how he'd broken your heart twenty-five years ago, I had to listen." He stopped for a moment and brought my hand to his lips. "He told me he lost twenty-five years because he didn't follow his heart. Then he told me I'd be a fool to do the same." He kissed my forehead. "You're one lucky girl to have a father and son who love you so much. I'd like to add my name to that list."

"Consider it done." I smiled.

If the flight attendant hadn't walked by, we would have faced each other unencumbered by the pesky seatbelts. But it was time to fly home. I took my eyes off him long enough to buckle up as he did the same. We were taxiing to the runway and would be taking off in minutes. I leaned into him laying my head on his shoulder as he held my hand in a way that felt like he would never let go. I gripped tighter, mostly because I loved this man with all my heart, but partly because I was still afraid of flying. As we took off, my mind wandered, imaging what the captain might say today.

"This is your captain speaking, Jamie. No, you are not going to die today—I've got this baby under control. Today is the day you can start to live again." The plane jerked as it steadied into its flight path causing my head to pop off Sam's shoulder and look out the window. I said a silent goodbye to Seattle as I pieced together the view of the city and the Sound through the sporadic buttermilk clouds. It had been a memorable homecoming, but Seattle wasn't my home anymore. Now, I was really going home.

Sam's voice brought me back to the real world. "Are you okay?"

"More than okay. I can get through anything with you. But I must admit, I'd rather be on the ground."

"Like maybe the beach?" His eyebrow rose, reminding me of his promise to be a sex addict with the one he loved.

"That would be nice. But seriously, Sam, how do you really feel about us? Do you still want kids?"

"I was hoping to have kids of my own, but we're over forty now. If you can let me share Justin, we won't have little kids holding us back if we want to travel or just stay in bed all day." The eyebrow rose again, along with something else, I think. He adjusted his shorts.

"Is that what you want?" I couldn't tell if he was letting his dream die or if he really didn't want, or need, to be a father.

"Sure," he said somewhat hesitantly. "I'm happy with you, Jamie. I don't need to pass on my DNA."

"But you have such great DNA, Sam. Any kid would be lucky to have your genes."

"Well, it's not important to me anymore. I want to be with you—just you and me. Let's celebrate with a plastic tumbler of fine airplane wine." He pushed the button to call the flight attendant.

"You might want to hold off on that request. I don't think I should drink."

"Oh, did you take a valium for the flight?"

"No, I can't do that either." As I studied his incredible loving eyes, I couldn't smile, I was a little worried.

"Why not? Are you sick, Jamie?" His smile faded as his eyes asked the question.

"Lovesick—that's for sure." I managed a feeble laugh. I swallowed hard knowing I had to tell him the truth. "Are you sure you want to give up your dream of having kids?"

He put both hands on my shoulders and stated his case. "To hell with kids, except Justin of course. I don't need to be changing diapers at my age."

"Then you're going to hate this news."

"What news?" He searched my eyes—eyes that could not hide any more secrets.

"If you want me, you're going to have to take all

three of us." I kept my gaze locked on his questioning eyes.

"Three?

"Me, Justin, and this little one growing inside me. Sam, you're going to be a dad whether you want to or not."

He had no words, but, oh, what a look.

And then he kissed me…

A word about the author...

Jacquie May Miller published her first article at age eleven in her neighborhood newspaper, the *Nosy Neighborhood News*. Many years passed before she was chosen as the featured writer in a literary journal produced at Washington State University where her short story, "Bernie's Choice," was chosen over many qualified submissions and published in 2013. It was recently republished on her blog.

Jacquie's first novel, *THE PRICE OF SECRETS*, is a work of women's fiction which explores the tenuous thread connecting family and a love left behind so many years ago. Secrets of the past will either break or strengthen that slim thread, but not without a price.

In addition to writing *THE PRICE OF SECRETS*, Jacquie has created May Daze, a blog exploring the value of friendship, family, and life's little surprises. You will find her at www.jmaydaze.com where she has attracted a loyal following from her Facebook and Twitter connections.

Jacquie lives in Washington close to her only child, Britt, who is the light of her life.

Thank you for purchasing
this publication of The Wild Rose Press, Inc.

For questions or more information
contact us at
info@thewildrosepress.com.

The Wild Rose Press, Inc.
www.thewildrosepress.com